BONE WALKER

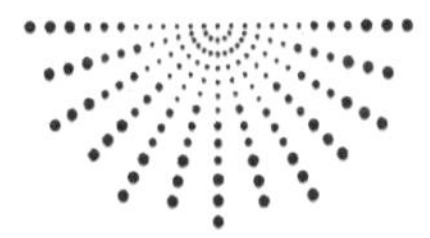

IDELLA BREEN

For Catherine & Jym

ALSO BY IDELLA BREEN

<u>The Dance of The Firefly</u>
When The Clock Strikes Nothing

<u>Fire& Ice:</u>
Blood Bound

Soul Awakened

Lover Eternal/Adventures of Elena the Werewolf

Pack Mentality

The King of Brimstone and Bones

<u>Blood & Ember:</u>
Blood Eternal: Book One of Salt

<u>Witch Twin Chronicles:</u>
Unrestricted Magic

<u>Eternal Soul Trilogy:</u>
Bone Walker

<u>Water & Bone:</u>
The Girl Who Leapt Worlds

<u>Novellas:</u>
Feeders and Bleeders

Descent

CHAPTER ONE

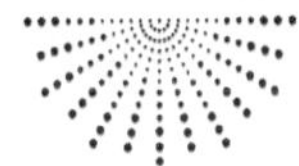

Sometimes, I felt like I drew the short straw in the game of life. Especially so on days like today, when I felt like nothing else could possibly go wrong. Then, it does.

The elevator doors closed in my face. The problem was that I wasn't on the elevator. No, I was standing in front of it with my cream-colored blouse untucked, a wrinkled gray skirt, all while holding one broken heel in one hand and my briefcase in the other.

"Shit!" I muttered in shock. This could not be happening. It's just not possible for this many things to go wrong before nine in the morning. I cursed under my breath again and looked at what floor the elevator was going to. Of course, it was going to the top floor. Why the fuck not!

I reached down and pulled the other heel off my foot, then pressed the call button for the second elevator. It was taking forever! I hopped from foot to foot. This garnered me some strange looks from other office workers, but I could not have cared less. This was crunch time, and I was late as fuck.

When the elevator stopped again, this time on the third

floor, I couldn't take it anymore. I raced off to the stairs. Looking up the barely used stairwell, I took a deep breath and adjusted my skirt. The things I did to keep my job. I managed to only stub my toe once, and only slightly rip my pantyhose on the way up, but my blouse had sweat stains on the armpits and my forehead was damp. By the third flight, I was panting and out of breath. I really needed to get into shape. Note to self: if I survive with my job today, get a gym membership.

I burst through the doors leading to the open space cubicles on the fifth floor, where I worked.

"Eliza! Thank God you're here!" a man in his early twenties yelled as he rushed over to me from where he had been standing by the water cooler. He took a minute to glance at me.

"What happened to you? You look horrible! You can't come here looking like that." He was twisting his hands back and forth as he fretted. Jacob had always been a nervous one. He didn't handle stressful situations well. *At least he could make it to work on time*, I thought belatedly.

I took a minute to catch my breath. "Just answer me one question, Jake; are they still here?" He continued to fret nervously with his hands, twisting them, but he didn't answer.

"Jake!"

"I'm sorry. They left, but they left their representative here to collect the information. I tried to stop them, but you're half an hour late, Eliza. They stayed as long as they could."

I deflated and leaned my back against the door. I could feel the familiar burn of tears stinging in the corners of my eyes.

"Shit!" I whispered.

"At least George hasn't—" He was cut off as a booming voice called my name. I felt my gut flip.

"Eliza, I see you finally made it to work."

"Double shit," I whispered and pushed off the door, turning to meet my boss, a graying man in his forties. George Crane was young for his position, but he had earned it through hard work and perseverance. I respected him a great deal, and he put up with most of my mistakes. I just hoped my luck hadn't run out yet.

"George, let me explain—"

"Come to my office, Eliza. We don't need an audience."

He motioned with his finger and pointed to the office on the other end, toward the back, past all of the cubicles.

"I'm sorry, Eliza," Jacob whispered.

I sighed and followed George. I felt like I was being led to the gallows as several people poked their heads out of their cubicles to watch me walk by. This wasn't my first fuck up. Actually, this was quite the habitual occurrence. But the sinking feeling in my gut warned that this might be the final straw, my last walk of shame.

I followed him into the corner office. Glancing to the left, I was met with a view of downtown Seattle in all its gray glory, outside a floor-length window. Turning back, I gave a cursory glance around the office; I had become familiar with it over the last month. The walls were painted a dark tan. Toward the back of the room was the typical dark wooden desk that was unnecessarily large, probably to make the person sitting in the guest chairs feel small. Companies were all about intimidation tactics. There were a few generic paintings on the front wall and a fake potted plant behind George's desk.

"Take a seat." George turned back and shut the door behind us. I did as directed and settled into one of the uncomfortable faux leather chairs. Gripping my broken heels and briefcase in my lap, I took a deep breath and waited to meet my boss's gaze as he sat. He sighed and massaged the bridge of his nose before looking up, his dark browns meeting my honey-green gaze.

"You've brought me to this, Eliza." His deep baritone confirmed my fears.

"Mr. Crane, I can explain—"

He cut me off. "I'm sure you have a very good reason for being late, but honestly, I don't want to hear it. I've listened to all of your excuses for this past month."

"But Mr. Crane—"

"No, Eliza. I've let you explain enough times. You've tested my patience time and again, but this time, I can't let you off with just a slap on the wrist. Look at you; you're a mess. Unprofessional. You knew how important today's meeting was. I had to personally kiss everyone's ass to make sure they would at least leave one of their representatives. But that is beside the point. I had someone clean out your desk. I want you to leave today. There is no tomorrow."

Even though I had expected this, I was still shocked that he had already cleaned out my desk. I felt the pang of betrayal. He had been waiting for me to mess up again and had been prepared to send me on my way when I did.

"Don't I at least get a week?"

"Usually, that would be the case. I would've given you the time to hand off your projects. But I've personally been training Jacob to take over your position, after your recent string of mishaps. He is more than ready to handle your projects and replace you. Today, Eliza. I want you gone today."

I nodded and stood, walking to the door. I paused and turned around one last time. "For what it's worth, I liked working with you, Mr. Crane. You were good to me."

He nodded, and I left the office. Like he said, my desk was

packed up neatly into one cardboard box. I dug through it and pulled out my extra pair of flats, for emergencies, and slipped them on before tossing my heels into the trashcan under my desk. With one last glance at my cubicle, I turned and marched out of a possible future.

AFTER SUFFERING THE STARES THAT FOLLOWED, ALONG WITH the whispers, I made the long trek through the office building. I wasn't free of them until I was walking along the sidewalk and making my way to the bus stop. I usually took the bus, as it would take me most of the way to my apartment, and I couldn't afford a car. It was still dark outside, as autumn was creeping up, and it looked like it was going to be another overcast day. I sighed and adjusted the box that was depressingly light. I had only been at the job for three months. The first month was all right, and the second month wasn't bad, per se, but the third month was one fuck up after the other, all leading up to today.

My mother used to joke about how unlucky I have always been. My life tends to do things in threes. Most of the time, it was harmless stuff; like the time I failed three exams in a row in college, even though I studied like crazy. Or the time I lost three baby teeth in one day after being hit in the face by a soccer ball.

It wasn't until my ninth birthday that it started to get bad. My mother died of breast cancer. Three years later, my older brother drowned in a lake. His foot got caught in lake grass. Three years after that, my dad died in a gang-related incident. All the police officer could tell me, as my life crumbled around me, was that my last living family member had been in the wrong place at the wrong time.

By the time I was fifteen, I was in foster care, as I had no living relatives that could take me in. So, for the first time in my life, I was alone in the world.

I was pulled from my thoughts when someone shoved into me, causing me to drop my box, spilling its contents all over the pavement. Why the fuck not!

"Watch where you're going!" a woman sneered at me before walking away. I felt my face flush and took a deep breath to prevent the tears and anger from bubbling over. Instead, I bent down, careful to fold my skirt appropriately so as to not flash any passerby. Of course, no one stopped to help me pick anything up.

I gathered everything and made my way to the bus stop. It was the only stop on my side of the street without cover, and as if I didn't already know that God hated me, just as I sat on the bench the sky opened up and it began to rain. It was only a light sprinkle, but it soured my mood even more.

I sighed and raised the box over my head. Luckily, the lights of the bus reflected toward me. By the time it stopped in front of me I was only slightly damp. I swiped my pass and took a seat toward the front, setting the box on my lap. I shuffled through the contents.

I pushed around some of the unimportant things until my hand brushed against the rough grain of a wooden frame; I pulled it out. It was a framed photo of my family. I'd managed to keep it despite some of my foster parents' attempts. It was ripped in some places, but the photo was still intact. The familiar burn filled my chest as I traced my fingers over my mother's face. I hardly remembered what she looked like anymore. If not for the photo, I wouldn't remember what any of them had looked like.

I had my mother's cocoa-colored hair and my father's honey-green eyes. My brother and I could have passed as twins when we were younger; we were only a year apart. My chest clenched as I studied the photo.

I wondered if they would be disappointed in me. This was the fourth desk job that I was fired from since graduating college. I wanted to do something that would make them proud if they were still alive, but all I was really good at was painting, and that would never pay the bills. I just wasn't good enough, despite what my best friend, Angela, was always telling me. My parents had been very left-brained, and even though they had never put down the value of the arts, they had never really talked about them at length, either. My father had always been too obsessed with finding a cure for breast cancer after my mother was diagnosed with stage three, meaning cancer had already moved to other places in her body. He was a leading expert in the field by the time she died, but he continued to work tirelessly in the labs until the day he was murdered.

Taking a shuddering breath, I set the picture down back into the box and looked at the other contents. There were a few miscellaneous knickknacks that were meaningless: a stress ball, paperweight, a couple of pens, a few paperclips, etc. I noticed they had taken back my work laptop. I could have used that. Like I said, I hadn't been there long enough to even settle in.

"Hey, sweet thing!" a deep voice called out.

I looked up and met the gaze of a man that looked to be in his late thirties. He had a dark-olive complexion, maybe Latino, and dark eyes. He was dressed casually, a thrift-store stock of clothing, and his ears were both pierced with silver studded crystals.

I quickly looked away and glanced at my watch. It was going on seven thirty in the morning. He might be from the night shift of one of the warehouses on the outskirts of downtown, or he was just looking for trouble.

"Hey, pretty lady!" he called out again.

I met the eyes of the bus driver, but he seemed content to turn back to the road. *Scumbag.*

"Nice pink bra, pretty lady. You putting on a show?"

Immediately, I looked down and saw that even though it hadn't rained that much, it had been enough to make certain wet spots on my cream-colored blouse see-through. I held the box in front of me tighter and glanced out the window. My stop was next.

"Want to go back to my place? I'll show you a nice time."

"That's enough of that!" the bus driver called out. I gave him a small smile. Maybe he's not a complete scumbag. The man remained quiet and the bus stopped. I stood and climbed off, shuffling the box into a more comfortable position on my hip. I lived in Belltown, in the low rent area. Naturally, there was a short stretch of abandoned buildings and businesses between the bus stop and the residential area. As a happy resident of Belltown, I was a tenant in the more artsy part on the outskirts of the city that was still under development. Several warehouses were only a block away from my apartment building.

I lived in the kind of place where a person locked their windows even if they were on the fifth floor. In the short stretch to my apartment, there were several streetlamps that I was thankful for, as I didn't want to trip on the cracked pavement. The rain was still a soft sprinkle, so there was hardly anyone out, making it even more ominous, as the moon was still high in the sky. Its luminous glory would peek out from behind the clouds to cast its glow in the dark morning hours.

I picked up my pace. I just wanted to go home to my warm apartment after a day like this. I had a bottle of Spanish red wine with my name on it to drown out my worries of whether I would make rent this month or if I was going to lose my heating again this winter.

It was then that I heard it. The sound of a second pair of sneakers slapping on wet pavement. A shiver of fear went down my spine. As I rounded the corner, I quickly glanced behind, only to see the man from the bus. My heart leapt into my throat as I picked up my pace. My apartment was only two blocks away. I glanced back again and saw the man come around the corner. *Shit.* Was he following me? Sure, I lived close to some warehouses. They were distribution centers. I'd know after the next block. He would have to turn left while I'd go right. He wasn't picking up his pace, but I was starting to get a stitch in my side from trying to keep up my brisk walk.

As I reached the next block, I turned right and continued off at my quick pace. Then, I heard it. He was running.

"Hey, pretty lady! You want to have some fun?"

I gripped my box and took off, running as fast as I could. My heart was pounding in my chest. *What do I do? I don't know how to fight. I work in a cubicle, for Christ's sake. Keep running. I should just keep running. Shit!*

My heart pounded and my sides hurt. *Keep running, Eliza, don't stop!*

"Hey!"

I was jerked back by my arm, dropping the box, scattering the contents.

"Stop! Let me go! Help!"

I felt it before I heard the slap, and stars flew before my eyes. I was dragged between two buildings and thrown up against a hard brick wall. A rough, calloused hand covered my mouth as hot, putrid breath fanned against my face. "I'm going to fuck your brains out!" he sneered and smiled, revealing yellowing teeth.

He leaned his full weight into my body, sandwiching me into the wall. I clawed out and managed to scratch his face before he gripped both of my hands in one of his and held them above my head.

"You bitch! You'll pay for that. I'm going to make this hurt," he sneered. That's when I felt something cold run against my stomach. He held a box cutter knife up for me to see.

"If you scream, I'll cut you so bad no one will recognize that pretty face of yours, understood?"

I could feel the wetness on my face letting me know I was, in fact, crying, even as I reluctantly nodded my head. This couldn't really be happening, could it? I'm not this unlucky, am I? Was I going to die? After everything I've been through, after all my hardships, I'm going to die in the most degrading way possible.

He released my mouth and my arms. The knife remained in one of his hands as he fumbled with the zipper of his jeans. I wasn't going to beg him not to do it. I wouldn't give him the satisfaction. No, I just had to wait until he let his guard down. I just had to endure. I've always endured.

As if he read my mind, he held the knife up to my neck. "No funny business, bitch," he warned. Then he trailed his hands up my legs and pushed up my skirt, slamming me against the wall, the knife biting into the soft flesh of my neck. I felt him rip away my underwear and I closed my eyes. Please, God, just let it be fast—

My thoughts were cut short as the man was jerked away from me, the knife biting deeper into my neck and dragging upwards before disappearing. I stumbled forward, nearly tripping.

"What the fuck!" I heard him yell. He then screamed, and I heard a sound like a stick snapping. My hand flew up to my neck where the knife had been and I pulled it away, revealing a line of blood. The crimson liquid trailed down my hand to my arms, along with the rain. In a daze I looked up, still trying to grasp onto what exactly was happening, and gasped. The rapist's arm, the one that had been holding the box cutter, was bent at an odd angle. *Broken,* I thought. But that wasn't the worst of it. He was currently being held captive by none other than the Grim Reaper.

The reaper pulled the struggling man forward, a mask of solid bone covering the entirety of its face. The rapist was forced to kneel before the god of Death, and I watched in rapt fascination and bated breath as the reaper bent down, forcing the man into a kiss. With my vision dimming, I wasn't sure if the gray light I saw being sucked out from the struggling rapist's mouth was my imagination or not, but as my body gave into the all-consuming insistence of unconsciousness, only one thought ran through my mind. Who knew the Grim Reaper was a woman?

CHAPTER TWO

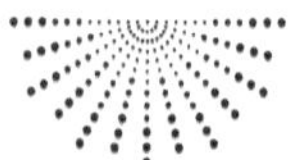

I woke to the godly smell of coffee, and surprisingly, it was mixed with the scent of burnt cinnamon. A curious smell. A familiar smell. Smiling, I stretched out on what I soon realized was the couch from my living room. It was a ratty old thing that I bought when I moved into my apartment. The family down the hall was moving out when I was moving in, and they couldn't figure out how to get the monstrosity down the stairs, as it wouldn't fit in the elevator. When I offered to take the lovely piece of furniture off their hands, they were only too happy to hand it over, for a small price. I'd been in love with it ever since. It was just the right amount of comfy and old that suited me just fine.

Why did I fall asleep on the couch? Was I working late again? As I sat up, a black leather jacket with silver lines running across the chest slid down off of me, and along with it, the strange but pleasant smell. I felt a sting in my neck and reached up, only to come in contact with the rough material that could only be gauze. What the—?

It hit me then. It was so powerful that I felt it with my

whole body, a physical jerk. It was like being hit by a bus. I began to shake uncontrollably, and a sound that could only be called animalistic escaped my throat. My fingers gripped the jacket until my knuckles turned white. I released another inhuman sound and pulled my knees up to my chest.

"You're safe now." A woman's soft voice cut through my shock-induced haze and I looked up, only to jerk back on the sofa. Standing at the end of the couch was the Grim Reaper from earlier. I had honestly thought I'd imagined the events that occurred before I passed out. It looked like I was wrong.

"What?" I gasped as I tried to hold myself together. It had to be a hockey mask or something. Halloween was coming up, after all.

"I said you're safe now. You're also in shock. Drink this."

She shoved a mug of coffee into my hands, making sure I had a solid grip on it before letting go and standing back, leaving a scent trail of burnt cinnamon in her wake. I looked down. It was my Garfield mug. The one Angela got me for my twenty-third birthday as a gag gift. She always said I was too lazy for my own good.

The warmth seeping through the mug brought me back to the present and my shaking began to slow. I took a drink and the heat of the coffee sliding down my throat helped ground me. After taking a few more sips, I set the mug down on the coffee table and sat back. I was only slightly surprised to see that the woman was studying me. Her gunmetal-gray eyes were watching me, through the holes of the mask, in a familiar way. I had a strange sense of déjà vu and a sudden warmth in my chest as our eyes met.

I cleared my throat. "So, are you going to tell me who you are?"

She didn't answer, and instead turned around and took a seat on one of the few chairs in my living room, across from me. She adjusted until she was comfortable before meeting my gaze again.

I guessed I'd have to begin this conversation. "My name is Eliza Trust. May I ask what your name is? I should probably say thanks for saving me. I'm sorry, I'm rambling. What's up with your mask, anyway? Is it like a Halloween mask or something? I'm going to stop talking now—"

I cut myself off as the shakes began to take over again. I shrank into myself, trying to slow down the adrenaline that was coursing through my body and to get my thoughts in order. Maybe drinking coffee hadn't been the best idea, but I knew that it was the only warm beverage I had in my kitchen. The woman wasn't helping with her eerie silent treatment, either.

"Eliza, why don't you go and take a shower? You're dirty."

A flash of anger bubbled up at her harsh comment and I shifted to give her a piece of my mind, only to feel a breeze on my nether regions. I gave a testing movement and realized I wasn't wearing any underwear. Blushing, I jumped up, only to stagger a moment before getting my balance.

I haughtily adjusted my skirt. "I'm going to take a shower."

The woman simply nodded and steepled her fingers while resting her elbows on the arms of the chair. I marched down the hallway and turned into the first door on the right, my bedroom. After retrieving some new underwear, a pair of relaxed fit jeans, and a long-sleeved, black shirt with the words Dare To Be Different printed in white lettering across the chest, I crossed the hallway to the bathroom.

The hot water helped with the shaking and to settle my irregular heartbeat. I took off the gauze and the spray from the showerhead stung the cut, trailing bloody water down into the drain. I would need to bandage it up again, I idly thought as I shampooed and conditioned my hair. I took a minute in the shower to just lean my head against the tiled wall, letting the boiling water cascade down my frame as the shaking began to subside completely.

What the hell was I doing? What was I going to do? I didn't even know anymore. I don't even know what to do next. That man—

I shuddered as I could still feel his calloused hands trailing up my legs. Anger spiked deep in my chest. I grabbed the bath sponge and vigorously scrubbed at my legs. I needed to erase the memory of his hands. I scrubbed them until the skin was pink and almost raw. The water stung it was so hot, and my skin was so tender.

What the fuck was I even doing? I was almost—

I slammed my hand against the tiled wall, a wet, fleshy sound resounding in the shower, only to be covered up by the sob that escaped involuntarily from my lips. I knew I was crying, even though the tears mingled with the water from the showerhead. The trembling began anew, and I sank to the floor clutching my legs to my naked chest. What was I even supposed to do?

I don't know how long I sat there, rocking back and forth, letting the water burn and wash away the pain and terror I had woken to, but it was long enough for the water to turn ice-cold.

Shakily, I eventually managed to pull myself up to turn off the water. I opened the window to let out what was left of the steam. Then, I climbed out of the shower and went to the sink. Wiping the condensation off the mirror, I was greeted with my reflection, and it left much to be desired. Pathetic would have been a compliment. My mascara ran down my face, making me look like a wet raccoon. I gingerly poked at the black bruise on the side of my face and winced. Not doing that again, I mused.

Taking a moment, I removed what was left of my

makeup. Grabbing a hairbrush from the basket above my toilet, I pulled it through my hair while sighing. Although my eyes were by far my unique feature, my hair was an entirely different story. It was dark brown, like mud, and was usually a pain in my ass to take care of. Even as I blow-dried it after finishing my shower, it had already begun to curl at the ends. The familiarity of the routine made sense, though. It helped because it was normal and right then, I needed normal.

I made quick work of taming the wild strands into a messy bun, and after getting dressed, I opened the door to the bathroom, only to pause.

The woman's voice echoed down the hallway in a distressed tone.

"I didn't mean to make contact, but I had no choice." She paused.

"Yes, I know it's too soon. I know, I'll handle it." Another pause.

"Yes, sir. Yes, understood. Goodbye."

Fear gripped my heart in its cold grasp. What did she mean when she said she would handle it? I closed the bathroom door quietly and stood back. I needed to think about this. I know the woman saved me, but should I really trust her? I mean, she could have done anything she wanted to when I was asleep, right? But that phone call didn't sound very reassuring, either. What if the "I'll handle it…" meant she was going to kill me? Maybe that's why she had been so quiet. She was deciding what to do with me next.

I glanced at the window behind me. I could probably fit through it. It would be a squeeze, but I'm pretty slight. I walked over to the window and slid it completely open. A strong gust of cold air blew into my face as I glanced outside. There was a fire escape just below it. Did I want to do this?

The memory of the gray light that came out the mouth of the rapist flashed in my mind, and I had my answer. I slipped through the window and settled barefoot on the fire escape, only making a little bit of noise. The cold of the metal sent a chill up my legs as it bit into the soles of my feet. I was wishing for shoes, even as I slowly walked down the stairs. When I made it to the last flight, I threw the ladder down. Just as I was climbing down, I chanced a glance up to my bathroom window and yelled, causing me to jerk in surprise, falling the last couple of steps to the ground. The sight of the woman in the skull mask looking down at me scared the shit out of me. I stood shakily, only to feel a sharp pain in my ankle followed by the sound of clanging metal as the Grim Reaper ran down the metal stairs.

"Leave me alone!" I yelled and tried to walk again, only to fall back down from the shooting pain up my leg. Of fucking course, I would sprain my ankle! Why the fuck not!

I had only managed to crawl to the end of the alley when I heard the slap of boots on concrete and the splash of a puddle.

I was almost there! Suddenly, I was grabbed and pulled into warm arms that held me almost protectively as the woman picked me up in a bridal hold. Naturally, I struggled.

"Let me go! Please! I don't want to die!" I babbled as I waved my arms wildly.

Absently, I could feel water dripping down my face. Whether it was from the rain or tears, I didn't know, but the woman managed to tuck my arms against her chest and carried me as I turned my head into her shoulder and wailed. The smell of burnt cinnamon filled my senses, and along with it, that same strange sense of comfort and a feeling of safety. I greedily drank the scent into my lungs, needing the feelings it evoked in me to settle my chaotic emotions, but fearing the woman that it came from.

I don't know how long it took but eventually, the woman was carrying me into my apartment, after unlocking my door with my key that she somehow magically produced from her pocket. She walked over to the sofa again, but instead of dropping me on it like I thought she would, she sat, still holding me in her arms, and pulled one of my throw blankets off the arm of the couch to wrap it around me. Her actions struck me as something odd for someone that was going to kill me to do, but this woman seemed to be all kinds of strange.

Now that we were out of the rain, I realized I was in fact crying. The soft murmurs of the woman holding me and the warmth of her body, along with the blanket, helped me settle once again. Afterward, I simply kept my face on her shoulder, gripping her shirt like she was the only thing keeping me grounded, which honestly, she probably was. It was a few minutes later when her soft voice filled the room.

"I'm sorry, Eliza. I didn't mean to scare you." She breathed deeply. "Shit, we weren't supposed to meet like this. I wasn't ready," she murmured.

I looked up, only to come face-to-face with the mask and her haunting, gunmetal-gray eyes peering down at me. This close, I was able to see that the mask fully encased her head, so that it was more like a helmet. I couldn't even see what color her hair was, but I could see that the mask was made of what could only be white bone. I reached up and ran my fingers along the contours of her cheek. Her eyes closed as I felt the cold, hard bone.

"Who are you?" I whispered.

Her eyes slowly opened again and I felt her cool breath fan gently over my face. The smell of burnt cinnamon was filling my lungs once again.

"My name is June West."

"June?"

She nodded.

"Are you going to kill me, June?"

I could see a flash of pain enter her eyes at my words as she shook her head. "No, Eliza. I'm not going to kill you."

"Then are you going to protect me?" I dared to ask, and even as the words left my mouth, the feeling of déjà vu filled me with such an intensity that it was almost painful.

It was a moment before she spoke, but her words carried a certain weight to them, as if she wasn't quite sure they were what she wanted to say.

"I'll do what I can, Eliza, but ultimately, the choice will be yours to make when the time comes."

I nodded slightly. "Why are you here? You seem to have made a mistake."

"I see you listened to my conversation. Is that why I had to chase you down the fire escape in the pouring rain?"

I blushed. "Well, you made it sound like you were going to kill me to cover up your mistake. I did what any sane person would have done."

June shook her head but when her eyes met mine, they held a lightness to them that hinted at a hidden humor.

"Protecting you will never be a mistake, and if given a choice to do it over, I wouldn't change anything. You're too important, Eliza, and it wasn't your time to die yet. You still have to make a choice."

"A choice?"

She seemed to jerk at my question, as if realizing she'd said too much.

"Never mind," June whispered.

"What choice do I have to make? What did you mean?"

She shook her head, but held me tighter. "It's not the time to discuss those things. The other side hasn't made a decision yet."

I pulled away from her slightly but forced her to meet my gaze. "June, tell me what's going on. You're confusing me."

But she shook her head again and moved to settle me on

the couch while wrapping me more tightly in the blanket. I let her put the physical distance between us, even though I felt the sting of rejection. June stood back and studied me once more.

"I have to go."

"Why?"

"Because, it isn't time yet. They aren't ready, and I made a mistake showing myself to you too soon. I have to go."

She moved to walk around the couch and I felt panic bubble up from deep within my chest.

"Don't go, June!" I yelled, but even as I stood to chase after her, I heard the slam of the front door. I hobbled over to the door and threw it open, but she was nowhere in sight. It was as if she simply disappeared into thin air.

As I closed the door and made my way back to the couch, I felt the panic settling inside and tearing everything to pieces. I moved to lay down but landed on something soft. Sitting up, I realized it was June's leather jacket. Desperately, I grabbed it and drew it to my face. The scent of burnt cinnamon filled me with a deep sense of peace and safety, the likes of which I hadn't felt since my family was alive.

I settled down on the couch and pulled the blanket up to cover me, as well as wrapping the jacket around my chest, and fell asleep in a state of panicked-bliss I hadn't felt since being sent to my first foster home. It was the mixture of panic from the uncertainty of the future and bliss in the thought that everything might finally be better. It was a state that would only ever last until morning, when the light of day would shine its harshness, illuminating the imperfections of reality. But for now, I would sleep restlessly and pray for a better tomorrow, where there wasn't so much fear and pain. I would pray for a tomorrow filled with hard gray eyes and soft arms, and most of all, the smell of burnt cinnamon and the peace it brought along with it.

CHAPTER THREE

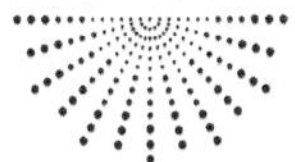

About a week after the incident, I was finally starting to get over my initial shock from the trauma of everything. I would still jump at loud sounds, letting me know I was nowhere near being completely over it, and I still had yet to leave my apartment. Instead, I holed up indoors and set up my easel in the kitchen, where it was easier to clean up the paint, and began painting. By the eighth day, I realized what exactly it was that I was painting, as I mixed the colors until they formed the same gunmetal gray that had haunted my dreams and were hidden behind the mask of the Grim Reaper.

Sometimes, I dreamt of her sucking the life out of me, like she did my rapist. I would imagine the way the gray light would be pulled from my body. Had that been his soul? Gray was such an unappealing color when it was his, but her shade was beautiful. It was the color of the ocean just before a storm, foreboding, a warning of the danger yet to come.

Other times, I remembered the gentle way she held me in her arms, and the same feeling of safety and peace would fill me until I woke back to the harsh reality. The reality was that

I was still too afraid to leave my apartment, but I wasn't going to let that stop me from painting. Actually, if anything, painting was exactly what I needed right now more than anything.

Some nights, I would think that I'd dreamt the whole thing. I was known to have an overactive imagination. Then, I would feel the genuine leather of the jacket she'd left behind, with the photograph of my family that I'd found tucked into the left pocket. Or, I would see the long, pink scar running from my collarbone up the right side of my neck from where the box cutter had dug into my skin, forever branding the memories of that event into my body. I would tremble as I traced the scar while looking into my bathroom mirror. I wanted to be stronger, but the ghost pain from both the event and the scar left as a reminder prevented me from moving forward.

So, instead, I would paint. It was a way of processing the event. It was my only solace, and had been so throughout my teenage years well into college. Once again, it was serving as a way to make sense of what had happened, for it had all happened so quickly, and some part of me still believed it was all a dream, despite the evidence to prove otherwise.

Some days, I wanted to hate my Grim Reaper. I needed to direct my anger at someone, but I had no one I was close to, and she had released so many emotions inside of me. It made me ask questions I didn't want to ask because she had suddenly just disappeared into thin air, leaving me confused, frustrated, and with more questions than answers.

Other times, I would mutter curses under my breath as I outlined her full-faced mask on my canvas and painted her haunting eyes that followed me into my dreams. At one point over the course of a month, I belatedly realized that I might be losing my mind. Then, I would laugh out loud and respond to my empty apartment, "I lost my mind years ago!"

I would then pick up a paintbrush and begin painting the contours of the bone mask.

Some days, I would entertain thoughts of what she looked like under the mask. Her voice had been delicate, and she had been softly spoken in the short amount of time I had spent with her; there had been an underlying strength to her voice that hinted at an authority that could be called upon when needed. So, I would trace strong lines of the mask, an angular jaw, the soft pale skin of her neck, and I would imagine that she was beautiful.

There were times that I felt like she was both my guardian angel and my tormentor, for leaving me so distressed and confused. By the end of the month, I'd completed my painting and cried myself to sleep for the last time. October had reached the end, and Halloween had passed. I was out of food and feeling like a caged animal trapped within the four walls of my apartment. It was time to rejoin the land of the living.

After taking a quick shower, which made me feel more human, I made my way into my living room. Picking up my keys and purse, I made a last-minute decision to grab the leather jacket on my way out the door. I'd been wearing it every day since the incident, and the unique scent of burnt cinnamon had since faded and been replaced by my own, but it still offered comfort that kept me grounded. Plus, Seattle was cold. If nothing else, it would keep the bite of the air from freezing me. I turned to lock my door.

"Going out, Eliza?" a light, airy voice asked.

I jump slightly but covered it up with a smile as I turned to address my neighbor, an elderly woman.

"Hello, Ms. Jean, yes, I'm going shopping for groceries. How are you today?"

"Oh, I'm fine here, just getting back from my daily walk around the block. It's been a brisk morning; you might want to pick up a pair of earmuffs while you're out. I hear from Trish that it's going to be a cold one this year."

I smiled. Trish was Jean's older sister. She lived on the third floor. They were close, and would go on daily walks in the morning, where I'm sure they caught each other up on the latest gossip of Belltown. Trish was nice enough every time I bumped into her in the elevator, if not a bit nosy. Jean and Trish were Belltown natives, born and raised in the same neighborhood as the apartment building they now lived in. I once asked Jean why she never moved away. The neighborhood was rough, and although I've lived in it for six years, I was young, and it was cheap, as well as close to the gallery I showed my paintings at. She had simply smiled and looked off into the distance before chuckling and saying, "Sometimes, you just can't escape a place no matter how hard you try or how much you want to. Some places just have a way of growing on you and becoming part of your identity. I couldn't move away even if I wanted to. It would be like ripping a chunk out of me. I just wouldn't be the same person, I suppose."

It had made sense in a wise way. The same way my living in the same building makes sense in an affordable way.

"It's always a cold one, Ms. Jean. But I'll be sure to pick some up while I'm out."

"You do that, dear," she called out as I made my way to the elevator. It was on my floor and empty as I entered it. I pushed the button for the lobby and leaned against the bar at the back. Should I take the bus? A shudder ran down my spine at the thought. The closest grocery store was more of a marketplace. I usually took the bus to get there and come back so I wouldn't have to carry the bags the few blocks it took to get home. The elevator dinged and the doors opened.

I needed the exercise anyway, and I wasn't planning on getting much. My wallet was depleted enough, and I doubted it would allow for much past milk and eggs, and maybe a coffee on the way home. Looking up into the sky, I calculated how much time I had before it would rain. The forecast said there was going to be a light drizzle between ten and twelve. I looked at my watch. It was only eight thirty in the morning. Just enough time, in my opinion. The market was only a few blocks away.

A light but brisk breeze ruffled my hair, and I paused to let it brush against my face and breathed the fresh air into my lungs. It was nice to be outside again. Four weeks holed up in my apartment may have been too long to be healthy. I took my time walking the few blocks to the market. About halfway there, the neighborhood turned from dilapidated grunge into respectable grunge, entailed by the art galleries and the painted murals on the sides of buildings. I stopped at several clothing stores to window shop and see the newest styles, taking note of the ones to stop back at once I got some fun money. I even paused for a few minutes in my favorite knickknacks and bobbles store and walked out with some more ideas for paintings.

By the time I reached the market I felt refreshed, and a normal part of society again. I made quick work of the market, managing to haggle a few good prices out of the vendors, allowing me to get a little bit more than expected, and began my trek back to my apartment with a small smile on my face. In fact, I was in such a good mood that when I walked past the coffee shop at the end of the market, I back-tracked and bought myself a double shot mocha latte.

It wasn't until I was walking out of the café that my bad luck kicked in. Just as I pushed the doors open and walked out onto the sidewalk, I was suddenly plowed over. I fell on my ass, dropping both my bags of groceries and my latte.

"I'm so sorry!" a deep voice called out.

"It's fine. I wasn't looking where I was going." I cursed as I saw my coffee. It was all over the concrete. I would have to buy a new one or just cut my losses and try again some other time. Instead, I began collecting my scattered food, only to be surprised when another hand reached for a bag of apples as well.

Finally, I looked up and was met with the profile of a handsome man. He was handsome in the boyish, good-looking kind of way and looked to be around my age, despite the baby fat still on his face. His beard gave him a few years. His light-blue eyes twinkled when he smiled and handed me the bag of fruit.

"Here you go."

"Oh, thank you." I gave him a small smile as I was brought out of my thoughts. We both stood at the same time. I was surprised when he held out his hand for me to shake.

"I'm Gabriel, by the way, but you can call me Gabe. Everyone does."

Surprised by the sudden introduction, I hesitantly shook his hand, pulling mine back quickly. Gabriel glanced down before meeting my gaze again.

"Sorry about your coffee. Would you like me to buy you another one?"

I glanced at the mess that was my drink and bent over to pick up the cup. I shook my head as I tossed it into the trash-can. What a waste.

"No, that's fine. I don't need another one. Thanks for the offer, though."

I turned around, only to jump back. Gabriel was too close for comfort.

"I insist."

I looked up from his broad chest and muscular arms and couldn't help thinking that if this guy wanted to hurt some-one, he could do so very easily. I shook my head and squared my shoulders despite the way my legs were beginning to turn to Jell-O.

"Really, it's fine. I don't need another one."

"Are you sure? I wouldn't mind." Gabriel moved closer, and I began to get the distinct feeling of being caged in. Suddenly, a strong gust of wind blew past and with it, the faint smell of burnt cinnamon. I watched as Gabriel stiffened and took a step back as a tight smile spread across his face.

"Maybe some other time then, Eliza."

I nodded dumbly and Gabriel gave a small, genuine smile, turned, then walked away. I watched him retreat down the sidewalk and cross over to the other side of the street. It was several long moments after he walked out of sight before I was able to shake off the feeling of the fear that had gripped my heart.

"Thank you," I whispered, sure my Grim Reaper would hear me, then I tightened the leather jacket around my shoulders and began my trek back to my apartment. I might need to move to a better part of town if I continued to get threatened by men. I had lived in Belltown for over six years. I'd moved here for the convenience of the art galleries, but now I was beginning to question if it was worth being so close to the galleries if I lost my life in the process, let alone my dignity. I took a deep breath, steadied my legs—they were still a bit wobbly—and walked onward. It wasn't until I was unloading my groceries that a frightening thought crossed my mind. I had never told Gabriel what my name was.

"This is amazing, Eliza. What do you call this piece?"

I smiled at Angela's enthusiasm. "*The Grim Reaper.*"

The Asian lady was nodding eagerly as her eyes panned over my painting of June.

"It's perfect! I'll add it to your other pieces for the show tonight."

"Thanks, Ang. Your excitement always makes it worth it."

Angela smiled widely at me. "You're so cute, Eliza; sometimes I just want to gobble you up."

I laughed. "What time should I show up for the show then?"

"It starts at six, so quarter till would be fine. I already set everything up over the weekend, and I have a few good people catering the event. Wine and cheese, again."

"Yum." I patted my belly.

"Oh, be quiet, you. I have to keep things up to a certain level of class while maintaining the artsy feeling and not being too stuffy. It's a fine line, the one I walk."

"Poor you." I smiled.

Angela laughed. "Do you need me for anything else?"

I shook my head. "No, I just wanted to drop off the painting."

"How's that corporate job you insist on keeping?"

I sighed. "I was fired."

Angela frowned sympathetically. "I'm sorry, Eliza. Look on the bright side. It's not like you need the money. Didn't your parents leave you a small fortune after they passed away?"

Angela was one of the few friends I had told about the money my parents left me. The money I refused to dip into. I'd met her in college, and we hit it off immediately in our shared Art History class. She was a Fine Arts major while I was just taking the class to fulfill the humanities for my Business major. We shared a passion for the arts despite the different paths we chose to take. My mom had been a lawyer, and my father, a prominent doctor, known for his research in breast cancer. It was almost an irony that the thing that took my mother's life was the very thing my father had set out to find a cure for. I was brought out of my thoughts when Angela poked me in the arm.

"You still there, space cadet?"

I laughed. "Sorry, what were you saying?"

"I was saying not to worry about the job because you already have the big bucks in your bank."

I sighed. "I know, but I want to make my own way in the world. I don't just want to live off the money my parents left me."

Angela leveled me with a look. "Honey, you have enough artistic talent to make it big if you just spend more time working the system."

"But I want to do a job that would make my parents proud. Being an artist has always been more of a hobby."

"Eliza, you have to get over this. Do you really think wasting away in a cubicle crunching numbers while you let all of your artistic talent atrophy would make your parents happy? You need to live your life for yourself."

I sighed again. "I know, Ang; I just don't know what to do anymore. Maybe getting fired from this last job is just a sign that I'm not cut out for that life."

"As well as the last four corporate jobs you were fired from."

"Way to rub it in."

"Tough love, baby. If I could paint like you, I would be making it big in New York and taking some hunky man to bed with me in between shows."

"Angela!"

"What! I'm a twenty-five-year-old woman. I'm not getting any younger, and neither are you. When was the last time you got laid? A year ago?"

I know she didn't mean to, but her question brought back the memories of that night; the ones I had managed to repress. A shudder went down my back and I instinctively grabbed my neck. Naturally, this caught Angela's attention.

"What's wrong with your neck?"

"Nothing," I said. I must have answered too quickly.

Angela frowned and grabbed my hand, pulling it back, and pushed aside the high collar of the leather jacket. Her face contorted in shock.

"What the hell happened to your neck?"

"Nothing, Angela. Just let it go."

"It looks like someone tried to cut a chunk out of it. There's no way in hell I'm going to let that go. Did your boss do this?"

"No! Mr. Crane was a good guy."

"Then who?"

"I really don't want to talk about it," I said as I glanced around at the few scattered people in the gallery. Sensing my hesitation, Angela grabbed my hand and dragged me through the employees only door, back into the storage area, shutting the door behind us.

"What happened, Eliza?"

"What if someone steals something?"

"I don't give a fuck. If you don't answer me in the next minute, I'm going to go to your office building to start tearing shit up until I get my answers."

"No! Fine, Jesus." I knew she would do it, too. Once in college, a professor had made an offhand sexist comment toward me, and Angela had tracked him down to give him a piece of her mind. She was suspended for a week for threatening a teacher, but I never forgot the feeling of having someone stand up for me for the first time.

"Well?"

Knowing there was no way out of this, I decided I just needed to say it quick. Like pulling off a Band-Aid.

"A guy tried to rape me on my way home after I was fired."

Angela's face went slack in shock, and I watched in rapt fascination as it flushed from her hairline, down her neck, and covering her chest, before disappearing under her shirt. Suddenly, she broke off into a string of what I know were Japanese curse words. There were a few F-bombs, and I think at one point she threatened to castrate a man with a rusty spoon. She waved her hands around, and I had to duck out of the way a few times to prevent getting slapped in the face. I waited until she calmed down and stopped waving her hands around like a maniac. She was breathing hard when she finally began speaking in English again.

"Did he succeed? Are you okay?"

I shook my head. "Someone showed up and pulled him off of me."

Angela pulled me into a tight hug. "Thank God," she whispered.

I held her just as tightly for a few minutes before we both pulled back.

"Do you need anything? Do you want to report it or did you already?"

"It's been taken care of," I said as I thought of the light being sucked from the man.

"Good."

I felt the sting in the corners of my eyes and was pulled into another bone-crushing hug.

"I love you, Eliza, you know that, right?"

"I love you too, Angela," I whispered.

She pulled back. "Do you want to stay over at my place? I know I have an annoying roommate, but I'm worried about you being alone."

"No, it's okay. I'm fine now. I've had time to process it all and I'm getting back into the swing of things."

Angela frowned. "If you're sure?"

"I am."

"Just so you know, there's always room for you at my place."

"Thank you, but I'll be fine."

"Okay."

There was a moment of silence before Angela pulled me into another quick hug, then led me back into the gallery. I wiped my eyes and followed her to the front of the store.

"Are you okay going home by yourself? If you want to hang around here until I close up, I can drive you home."

"It's okay. I don't live far from here, and I don't want it to stop me from living my life. I don't want to live in fear."

Angela smiled. "You're a strong woman, Eliza; don't let anyone tell you different."

"Thank you, Ang. I'll see you tonight."

"Be safe."

"I will. Bye."

CHAPTER FOUR

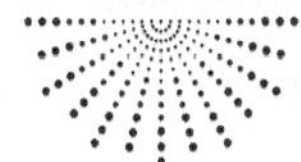

I spent all day cleaning my apartment of the dust and dirt that had collected during my month-long vacation. By six, I was mingling with the guests and patrons at the gallery. It wasn't until an hour into the show that I had managed to get my first glass of wine and finally got a moment to myself where I wasn't either kissing ass or receiving praise.

Without really thinking much about it, as my mind was a jumbled mess and numb, I found myself standing in front of the painting I had done of June. I was once again caught in the gunmetal gaze, as if in a trance, when I felt a presence come up next to me. I glanced to my right, only to be shocked at the beauty of the man standing next to me. When I say beauty, I mean, the man next to me was drop-dead gorgeous, in the dark knight kind of way. He had a chiseled jaw and a dark complexion that made his features all the more charming. His hair was black, and when his gaze met mine, I found myself staring into eyes as black as an abyss. He smiled, showing off white teeth that would make any dentist proud.

"Hello, are you the artist, Eliza Trust?" His voice was smooth as silk.

I nodded, still trying to find my voice, as my mouth was dry all of a sudden.

"I'm Kaleb Cole, and I'm honored to be here to see your artwork."

"Thank you," I murmured, and blushed slightly.

"I should be thanking you. But, I'm sure you're tired of all the flattery."

He held out another glass of wine toward me and I glanced down at my own, now empty, glass.

"Thanks." I took the offered drink. He smoothly took my empty one and placed it on one of the servers' trays as they walked by.

"Would you mind my asking what inspired this painting?" He gestured to the portrait of June.

I looked at it, feeling guilty for some reason, then shrugged.

"I ran into the Grim Reaper recently when I had a brush with death; this is the result."

"The Grim Reaper?" He chuckled a dark sound that reverberated from deep within his chest. "I'm sure she would enjoy that name," I thought I heard him whisper, but before I could ask him about it, he continued.

"What are your views on death, if you don't mind my asking."

"Why?"

He smiled, but something about the glint in his eyes sent a shiver down my spine, and not in a good way. I got the distinct feeling of this man being dangerous in the way a flame is dangerous if I were to play with it. "Please, humor me."

I nodded before looking back at the painting and

collecting my thoughts. "I like to think something amazing happens when we die."

"Why do I feel like there is a 'but' at the end of that sentence?"

I glanced at him. "Well, I guess that's because sometimes I feel like there's nothing at the end of it all."

"What makes you think that?"

I turned back to the painting. "Probably because sometimes I feel like Heaven and Hell are already on Earth."

I could feel his heated gaze burning holes into my head, but when I turned to meet it, he was looking down at his now empty wine glass. He looked up and smiled.

"What if I told you that you might be right?"

I frowned. "About what exactly?"

"About Heaven and Hell being on Earth? What if I told you that I was a demon come to claim your soul?"

The feeling of reality slipping through my fingers engulfed me as I studied the man next to me, trying to decide if he was crazy or telling the truth. But there was no way he was telling the truth, right? Right?

"I guess I'd have to tell you that you could only have it if you pried it from my cold fingers because I have no intention of giving my soul to a demon no matter how handsome he thinks he is."

There was a brief moment of stillness as my answer hung between us. The sound of the people around us seemed to fade away as I was pulled into the darkness of his eyes. They seemed bottomless, and hypnotizing, almost smothering. I jumped as his deep laugh burst forth. He turned and swept another glass from a server's tray and held it in the air.

"A toast then. To the beginning of the end. May the best man win."

Hesitantly, I nodded and clinked my glass against his, watching as he drank the wine in a few quick gulps.

"But I'm not a man."

He smiled. "No, you're not. Call it a figure of speech. I'm sorry to say that I must go now. I've gone past my allotted time. I may have said a little too much, too. I imagine I'll get a slap on the wrist for bad sportsmanship."

I frowned. "I don't understand."

"In time you will. I'll see you around, Eliza. It was a pleasure."

"Okay?" I whispered as I watched him walk away and melt into the crowd only to disappear.

"That wasn't weird," I muttered and took a drink from my glass, emptying it in the process. The sense of wrongness still lingered even after Kaleb had left and I hoped the wine would help erase it.

"There you are, Eliza!" Angela pushed through the crowd, towing a small, balding man behind her.

"Eliza, meet Henry," she introduced.

I shook his hand absently, still trying to process the strange encounter I had just had.

"It's a pleasure finally to meet you, Ms. Trust. Angela has told me so much about you."

"The pleasure is mine."

"Eliza, Henry is the director at Philo's." Now that caught my attention. Philo's was one of the big five galleries in Seattle.

"It truly is a pleasure then," I smiled.

"I would love to speak with you sometime about having your art shown at my gallery. I've been a fan of yours for quite some time now."

A bubble of excitement filled my gut. "I would be truly honored, Henry."

"Good." He pulled out a business card and a pen. After scribbling on it a moment, he handed it to me.

"That is the number to my office. I only give it out to

promising talent. Call me, and we will work out a time to meet."

I took the card, my heart pounding in my chest. "I don't know what to say."

"Don't say anything. Just paint me something for your future show."

"Thank you."

"Don't mention it. Now I must be going. I'm late for another meeting. Think about it, Ms. Trust. And give me a call sometime next week."

"Yes, sir."

Henry paused and glanced up at the painting of June. "Truly magnificent," he seemed to say to himself before he turned back to me.

"Good night, ladies."

I watched Henry go back into the crowd—it seemed to swallow him whole—before turning to Angela, who had a shit-eating grin on her face.

"Am I good or what?"

"How did you…" I trailed off.

"He's been coming to the gallery for months now, and I've been dropping hints that you'd be willing to show at other galleries. When I told him about the show tonight, he said he would be here, but I didn't want to say anything and get your hopes up."

"Thank you, Ang. I don't think you know how much this means to me."

She smiled and pulled me into a hug. "Believe me when I say that I do."

We separated.

"Just promise me one thing, Eliza?"

"Anything."

"Promise me that, no matter what, you will call him."

I paused. "What do you mean?"

"I mean, when you wake up tomorrow, don't let your logical mind talk you out of this once-in-a-lifetime chance."

I nodded. "I'll call him, I promise."

She squealed and pulled me into another hug. "Congratulations then."

I smiled. Maybe my luck was finally beginning to look up for once. I looked past Angela's shoulder only to meet the gunmetal gaze of June, my Grim Reaper, and the feeling of foreboding settled heavily on my shoulders.

"LIE TO ME," I DEMANDED.

"What?" June asked, even as she sat down next to me on the damp sand.

"I want you to lie to me."

"Why?"

I gave her a small smile as I adjusted the bangles around my wrist. I seemed to be wearing strange clothing that was from another time. I was dressed in simple clothes, but I was decorated extravagantly with jewelry. I met June's gaze. I seemed to have no control over my body or the words coming from my mouth. "Because lies are beautiful sometimes."

She shook her head. "Don't you want the truth? It's all that matters."

I turned to look out at the ocean as the waves crashed into each other. I had the distinct knowledge that the sun would be rising soon. "You're wrong."

"How so?" Her brows bunched adorably.

"There is no such thing as the truth. The truth is shrouded in opinions and biases. The truth is an illusion, an ugly lie. I want you to tell me a beautiful lie, because the thing I want to hear in my last moments is something that will remind me of the love we could have had. I know the facts. The facts tell me that I am dying. That it's my destiny to die this way. I am the Lamb of Essence. It is my birthright to die. The facts tell us that we failed to defy fate this time. But, facts are mortal, while lies transcend time and space. Tell me something beautiful, and it may come true in my next life."

June met my gaze; I could make out her gunmetal-gray eyes belying the pain of her failure, despite being unable to discern the definite features of her face. It was like I could see her without really seeing her. I smiled sadly even as she spoke. "I don't know what to say."

"Tell me you love me. That you have always loved me, and that when I'm gone, you will use that love to move forward in life. To move and find love again."

Tears trickled down her face. She furiously wiped at them. "I'm not good at lying."

I smiled a true smile. "That in itself is a beautiful lie. Tell me more."

She nodded and reached for my hand, taking it into her warm grasp. "I…I love you. I've loved you since the first time I laid eyes on you. I don't think I ever stopped loving you and I don't think I ever can. You take my breath away every time you smile. My heart flutters every time you laugh. But the greatest lie of all is that I have always been yours, and I always will be."

I nodded even as my eyes stung. I took a deep breath. I had to be strong. "There, that wasn't so hard now, was it?"

June sobbed. "I think I hate you right now."

I shook my head and gave a small laugh. "This is not the time for truth. You can say that when I'm gone. You can talk about all kinds of truth then, but right now, we are in the time of lies. Tell me something else."

"I can't live without you," she whispered.

I nodded. "You will, though. You'll move forward, and one day, you'll forget me. I'll be a faded memory, a smell or a sound that you only vaguely recall for a moment before you continue with your day—and that's okay. That's the way it should be."

"No! That won't happen!"

I chuckled. "You're getting good at lying."

She shook her head. "I don't like this game."

I looked back out at the ocean. The first rays of the new day were beginning to peak above the horizon. It was time. "I know. Why don't you just hold me for a while, then? I think I'd like that."

June nodded and pulled me into her arms, wrapping them tightly around me, letting me settle against her soft chest.

"You can sleep for a while if you want," she whispered.

"I think I'll do that. Wake me up if I start snoring."

She chuckled even as it turned into a sob. "I will."

"I love you too, by the way. Just wanted you to know that."

June nodded. "I know."

"Good…" I trailed off as I felt my whole body go slack, relaxing into her strong and steady hold. I felt my heart stutter as the first rays of morning shone on my eyelids. Then, darkness claimed me. The side I had chosen this time was the demons' side. I chose it to spite the light for denying me the love I so desired. June stood by my decision as she had in every lifetime, and I believed, she would continue to in the lifetimes yet to come. She was on my side no matter what side I chose, and for that, I was forever grateful because the truth was that I would be alone if it weren't for her. She was mine, even though I could never be hers.

I felt myself leave my body and enter June's. Her thoughts flooded into my mind as I became one with her.

JUNE LOOKED OUT INTO THE DISTANCE EVEN AS SHE FELT THE life leave the body held tightly in her arms. The fact was that the soul she had held in her grasp, the woman, her woman, was a victim of fate. They both were, but the beautiful lie was that they were soul mates. The truth, though, the truth was too much to bear even for her, a bone walker. The truth was that they were never meant to be. It was a biased and opinionated truth that she was determined to prove a fallacy.

June watched the sun rise high into the sky and watched the waves crash against the sandy bank. No one was there to tell her to stop the tears from falling; no one was there to tell her beautiful lies. All she had to hold her over until the next rebirth of the Lamb of Essence, the woman of many names and lives, all of them tragic until the very end, her lover, were the lies and the memories of all the times she had failed. But most of all, she had the hope that there would be a day, a time, a moment, when she finally broke the cycle, and that would just have to be enough because the fact was, she had no other goal in her immortal death but to set her lover free.

<hr>

"JUNE!" I GASPED AS I SAT UP IN BED. I PANTED HEAVILY, trying to slow my racing heart. What the fuck had that been about? What kind of dream was that? Was I losing my mind?

My thoughts continued to race, the silence of the room only interrupted by my irregular breathing and the beating drum of my heart. Why did I have that dream? It had felt so real, almost as if I had lived it; but that was impossible. I didn't even know what the woman looked like. Even in my dream, she was shrouded in a fog. Just an after-image, the thought of an image, but not enough substance to make out anything more than the softness of her voice and the overwhelming familiarity; the fondness I would usually only feel for a loved one, all directed at a woman I didn't even have a face to relate to.

I wiped the sweat from my forehead and pushed the covers off. I just sat for a moment, with my feet touching the wooden floors of my bedroom, before I reached over and turned on the lamp on my bedside table. The soft, yellowish light illuminated the familiar space that I'd known as my room for the better part of six years. I was proud of it and the hominess it supplied. It was me, and it was mine. I had never had my own room growing up. Most of the foster families I was shuffled through always had at least three to four children moving about the place. I was always forced onto the top bunk of a more-loved daughter.

Most foster families balk at the idea of taking on a teenager almost done with high school. Most people want a baby or a small toddler. A blank slate. Teenagers in foster care have too much baggage, were too much work, and not enough time to reprogram them to fit into the new family before they were considered adults. I'm sure most were thinking, why bother?

But there were some that had teenagers forced on them, or others that simply took them in for the paychecks we brought with us. They weren't necessarily bad people, those families. They just lacked privacy—and most importantly, they lacked love. It was hard to find a family that would love a child that wasn't theirs unconditionally. That's not to say they didn't exist, but more to say that they were hard to find. I only found one toward the end, and I was already being shipped off to college on a full academic scholarship. I lost touch with my foster family, and during my third year in college, I found out through the grapevine that they had died in a horrific house fire that year. I couldn't help but feel like it was my fault. If it hadn't been for Angela, I wouldn't have pulled through and graduated. I didn't even have any photos of the woman that had helped me through high school.

And now, here I was, in a room that I could call my own, surrounded by the essence of the things that helped define me in some way, dreaming about a woman I didn't even know. I sighed. What was wrong with me? I had felt so much longing as I asked her to lie to me. So much pain; and it had felt like my pain. Like a scar that reopened and wept anew. But, I don't remember that ever happening to me. I think I would remember a woman like June. The Grim Reaper getup would ensure that. Besides, I had felt other things in that dream that I wasn't quite ready to analyze.

I stood and felt my pajamas cling to me. Ugh, gross, sweat. Okay, first a shower, then a glass of water, then back to bed. I glanced at the digital clock on the table. Three in the morning? Of course it was. I sighed and stood. My throat felt scratchy. Maybe I should get that glass of water first. I stood, but suddenly lost my balance and fell back onto the mattress. My legs felt weak.

"That dream must have affected me more than I thought," I whispered.

I attempted to stand again and was successful. I left my bedroom and crossed into the bathroom across the hall. There was a plastic cup that I usually used to rinse my mouth with, sitting there on the sink. I filled it with water from the tap and greedily drank from it. Once I had enough, I pulled out a towel and undressed from my sweaty clothing before climbing under the still warming spray. An hour later, I was climbing back into bed feeling calmer and more relaxed.

Sleep claimed me quickly, the shower having wiped away most of the lingering memories of the strange dream. There were no more strange dreams that night, just blissful darkness until the morning light of the next day woke me; but by then, all thoughts of the dream were long forgotten.

CHAPTER FIVE

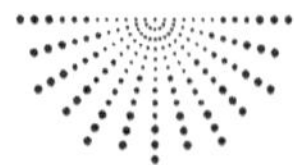

The rest of the week flew by without event. I called Henry, after several attempts at talking myself out of it, despite my promise to Angela. If it weren't for her endless insistent badgering, I would have never got up the nerve to call and make the appointment. I had made a few halfhearted attempts with some pencil pusher jobs, but hadn't received any calls back going into the next week. Without much thought, I soon found myself being shown around Philo's on a Tuesday afternoon by Henry and another director that was lackluster at best.

The gallery was large, but that was to be expected for the area it was located in. Philo's was located in Queen Anne, one of the most affluent neighborhoods of downtown Seattle. The gallery was two stories and a basement that housed some of the more temperature-sensitive art pieces. The walls were a bleached white to offer the perfect canvas for the artists to display their work and not take away from it. At the entrance, there were two options in which to proceed. If a person turned left, they were taken down a hallway of some of the most modern art Seattle had to offer. That hallway took the person in a roundabout that would lead them through several rooms, all filled with varying works of art ranging from prosthetic leg lamps to rusty cars painted with unicorns. Going that way, a person would eventually end up at a winding staircase where they were given the choice of going up or down.

Going up would lead a person to the Heaven Room; a room devoted to celestial works depicting the beauty of angels in all their benevolent light. The room itself was filled with natural light along with many ceiling lights. Just walking into it, I felt like I was in someplace holy. Some of the paintings depicted the holy ranks an angel could achieve in their lifetime, as well as the miracles they would bestow upon humans. It was as beautiful as it was intimidating.

Going down the staircase was something completely different. It would lead a person to the Hell Room, which was filled with demonic statues and the gallery's most prized possession, a painting named *The Fall of The Morning Star*. It was a painting that was as beautiful as it was vicious. The painting depicted what looked to be an angel, having his wings torn off by other angels. What made it beautiful was the care the artist took in painting the details of the wings. They were so lifelike that I felt that if I touched the painting, I would feel their softness, like touching an eagle's feathers. It was vicious because of the gruesome display the other angels were enacting. It would have been kind to say it looked like it hurt. The agonizing pain the fallen angel must have felt during the process was beyond human compre-hension.

"What do you think of it, Ms. Trust? Is it not amazing?" Henry asked. His voice held hints of the awe he must feel every time he laid eyes on the painting.

"Who is the Morning Star?"

Henry didn't even look away as he answered. "Morning

Star is the meaning of the name Lucifer. It was Satan's name before he fell from heaven. Isn't it beautiful?"

I studied the painting. Honestly, I didn't know what to say. It brought to mind the conversation I'd had with Kaleb at my show, and it made me realize that I didn't particularly conform to any religion. Despite the despair and the hardships my life brought to me, I had never turned to a Higher Power to fill my heart and grant me hope that many religions do. Instead, I became more independent and if anything, one could say I had turned my back on the stability religion grants. I was alone, and I was okay with that. I didn't need a god to save me because, in a way, I was already damned.

"Ms. Trust?" I was brought out of my thoughts by Henry touching my shoulder.

"I asked what you thought of the painting, but I can already see you are as in awe of it as I find myself every time I see it. Let us continue then. There is still much to show you."

I nodded and followed him back to the staircase. Henry continued with his tour, now showing me what happens should a person have turned right at the entrance to the gallery.

"By going right, we are led to this room."

We entered a room where all the walls were painted earthy tones instead of the whites that most of the gallery was colored in.

"What do you call this room?" I asked as I took in the sculptures of women with butterfly wings and paintings of what could only be gnomes, along with other fantasy creatures.

"We call this the Earth Room. We have filled this room with art depicting the mythology humans have created throughout time. You can find anything from vampires and werewolves to elves and trolls here. Following this way, a person will be led through an empty room that we are still working on, then to the same staircase that leads up to the Heaven Room or down to the Hell Room."

I studied the room once more, taking in the butterflies and the lightness it presented compared to the previous two rooms. The other director had excused himself by now, saying something along the lines of needing to attend to certain business. I followed Henry back to the entrance and into the lobby. He made a sweeping motion with his hands as we finished the tour. "So, what do you think, Ms. Trust? Does Philo's meet your standards?"

I'm not afraid to admit that I was in complete awe of the place. Naturally, most of the customers were rich people, and one thing all my cubicle jobs taught me was that if you please rich people, you get notoriety and money. Money wasn't my main goal but to become well-known in the artist circle, a more exclusive club, was tempting. Honestly, I'd never had much confidence in my art. Like I told Angela, it was more of a hobby. I was just lucky that I happened to have a talent for it. I'd never seriously considered pursuing a career in it— until now.

"Most definitely, Henry. This place is amazing. I'm honored you believe my art is worthy of decorating the walls and rooms here."

"Nonsense! You are an amazing artist. One of the best talents in the last five years. As you know, I've had my eye on your work for some time now, and you have proved time and again to consistently produce quality work."

I could feel the heat of a blush on my cheeks. "You flatter me."

"It's not flattery if it's the truth. So, I take it you're interested then?"

"Yes, sir."

"Excellent. I'll have Jess tell my lawyer to draw up a

contract to have you sign. We would need to schedule a day for both of our lawyers to be present at the signing. Is that acceptable?"

"Yes, sir."

"Perfect! I have your number now. We will be in touch within the next few weeks. I want to begin planning a show for next year as soon as possible."

I nodded while he continued to ramble on as we walked to the exit. *I can't believe this is happening!*

"I have just one question, though," I asked as I thought of the empty room.

"Yes, my dear?"

"Where exactly would my art fit in? Most of what I create deals with the realities of life and death, but I explore more of a liberal view of the eternal life of a soul as opposed to its being laid to rest in some celestial or demonic eternity."

He nodded, a smile spreading across his lips. "Yes, indeed. You are correct, Ms. Trust. I have big plans for your art. I have been working on a project; you remember the empty room?"

"Oh?"

"I call it, The Eternity Room."

I nodded. "Yes, I think my art would suit that type of room better."

He smiled. "I thought you would. Do you have any other concerns?"

I shook my head.

"Good! I will walk you out then."

"You don't have to do that."

"Nonsense! I was raised a certain way, Ms. Trust. Let this old man continue with the chivalry I have had beaten into me since boyhood."

I smiled. "Okay."

He winked before leading me to the exit. Henry opened

the door for me, and I moved past him only to collide with something solid. Strong arms wrapped around me, preventing me from falling, and steadied me before letting go.

"We meet again!" a good-humored voice said.

I looked up and met the sky-blue eyes of Gabriel. "Gabe?"

He laughed. "The one and only."

"Have you met Gabe?" Henry asked.

"I've already had the pleasure of meeting Eliza." Gabriel grinned.

Henry smiled. "Is that so? Small world, I suppose."

"I guess," I murmured as I fixed my jacket that had bunched up from the almost fall.

Henry continued. "Gabriel Johnson the third is one of our gracious patrons."

"A patron?" I asked as a sinking feeling filled my gut.

"Henry, you're embarrassing me," Gabriel responded good-naturedly as he slipped his hands into the pockets of his black slacks.

"Nonsense. It's because of your support that Philo's has prospered in the last five years."

Gabriel shrugged. "I do what I can."

He turned back to me. "Why are you here, Eliza?"

Henry cut in before I could even open my mouth. "Ms. Trust is one of our new artists. It's not official yet, but I have big plans for her."

"Is that so?" He smiled, attempting to show off his boyish charm.

"Yeah." This was not looking good for me.

"What a coincidence," he chuckled.

"I guess," I said.

"Maybe we could get together over a drink sometime and talk about art. I still owe you a coffee, don't I?"

"Don't worry about it," I frowned.

The double doors swung open and a woman in a pencil skirt popped her head out. "Mr. Smead? You've got a call from a client on line two."

Henry grinned, "Oh yes. I was expecting them to call soon." He grabbed my hand and shook it excitedly.

"We'll be in touch, Ms. Trust. Keep painting. If all goes well, in a year's time, you'll be the talk of Seattle."

"Thank you, Henry." I pulled my hand back.

"Good day, Gabe. Why don't you walk Ms. Trust to her car and fill her in on how the gallery works?" He winked.

"That's not necessary—"

"That's a great idea," Gabriel said, and before I could say anything else, Henry was gone, and I was left alone with Gabriel.

"Great," I murmured under my breath.

"Should we go?"

"You really don't need to."

"I want to."

"Fine!" I said exasperatedly, because apparently, nobody cared about what I wanted.

I started walking toward the bus stop. I just hoped that once he realized that I didn't have a car, he wouldn't try to drive me home. The last thing I wanted to do was fuck up this opportunity by pissing off one of the gallery's patrons. He followed behind me in silence for a few moments before my arm was suddenly grabbed and I was forced to face him.

"Are you just going to ignore me?"

"That was the plan!" I yelled as my gut clenched in irrational fear.

Gabriel frowned. "I think we got off on the wrong foot, Eliza. I don't know what I did to offend you, but can we start over again?"

"Let go," I said between gritted teeth.

His features lit with surprise and he immediately

dropped my arm. I didn't let it show, but my heart was pounding in my chest as images of the last time a man grabbed that same arm filled my mind. I couldn't help the glare I directed at him for making me remember that morning and the events that took place on my way home from work. I took a deep breath. He didn't know. I really shouldn't hold it against him; plus, it would only benefit me to play nice with the rich boy. I knew Henry was in love with my art, but I hadn't signed a contract yet, and I was pretty sure he was more in love with the rich patron that's keeping his gallery open. Artists were a dime a dozen; patrons were gold.

Once again, I straightened my leather jacket. I knew it was a mistake when Gabriel's eyes suddenly widened before turning hard. He reached forward and roughly pulled back the collar of my jacket.

"Hey!" I pushed him away.

"What happened to your neck?"

"That's none of your damn business!"

He grabbed my arm again, gripping it almost painfully tight. "I asked you what happened to your neck."

"Let me go! Or I'll scream!"

"Tell me what happened to your neck." His voice rose with each word and his grip on my arm tightened.

"You're hurting me!" I tried to pull my arm free, but his grip was iron.

"Just tell me what—"

A soft voice interrupted whatever he was going to say. "Let her go, Gabriel."

He dropped my arm immediately. My heart fluttered in my chest when the woman spoke again, but this time, there was a dangerous edge to her voice as well as a definite command. "I think you should go into the gallery. I'll take Ms. Trust home."

I still hadn't turned around. I think I was afraid that if I turned around, she might disappear again.

"This doesn't concern you, soul stealer."

"I can always demand another representative from your side. Despite what you may think, you aren't entitled to the position," came the soft reply.

Gabriel sneered, "My Father will hear of this; I guarantee it."

"Understood. He will also hear from me how rough his son was with Ms. Trust—and if there are any marks, I promise you that there will be severe punishment."

I watched as his face darkened even as it paled. Then he turned around and stormed off like a petulant child. A soft hand settled on my own and I was gently pulled away from the bus stop and toward the parking lot. Finally, I was forced to turn to my savior but she was facing away from me, so all I was able to see was her platinum-blonde hair that fell like a waterfall down to the middle of her back. It was so light it almost looked white, but it shone like gold when the light from the sun hit it just right.

We paused in front of a black Camaro. "Get in." Her voice was so soft, it was like the whisper of the wind.

I climbed in without complaint and immediately turned to inspect her features when she settled down in the driver's seat. My imagination couldn't hold a candle to the real thing. She started the engine as I studied her profile. She was beautiful in a sinful way. Her narrow nose sloped down to pink lips. The top lip was thinner than the bottom, which she was nibbling between her teeth. Her face broke from high cheekbones down into a strong jaw that slanted down to a long, pale neck. Looking back up, I gasped as I met the gunmetal-gray eyes that had haunted my dreams.

"June," I whispered.

Her brows bunched adorably before she turned back to

the road. I was breathing in greedy lungfuls of the burnt-cinnamon-scented air that filled the car like a perfume when she spoke again. It was so quiet I almost missed it.

"Are you okay, Eliza?"

"June, what's going on?" I asked.

Her brows bunched again and her features contorted in obvious pain before she turned back to the road. We sat in silence, and I turned my gaze to look out at the scenery whipping by us. She obviously didn't care about the speed limit. I sighed.

"What are you thinking about?" she asked.

"I don't know. I guess I'm just really confused and really pissed that I'm so fucking unlucky."

"It's not your fault."

Anger spiked so hotly in my chest that I couldn't stop myself. Everything just spilled out as if I had no control over my mouth.

"What the fuck do you know, June? Nothing! You don't know one damn thing about me. No one does. I'm just not meant to be happy. God must hate me. I must be cursed. Everyone I've ever loved has died on me! Whenever something good starts to happen in my life, some Higher Power swoops down and says, fuck you, before pulling the rug out from under my feet."

I was yelling and screaming. Fat, hot tears were streaming down my face, but I just couldn't stop. It was like the dam had finally burst. I just couldn't do it anymore. I couldn't suffer in silence.

"And you know what? I honestly really wanted to do the gallery thing. It would've been a dream come true, a dream I had never let myself have before because I knew that if I lost the one thing that has kept me sane all these years, I might finally break. I just didn't think I could handle that. I can't handle it. Look at me! Just fucking look at me! Why am I even alive? Is it my purpose in life to be shit on again and again? Why me? What the fuck did I ever do to anyone to deserve this life?"

I finally stopped, panting, gripping my hands into fists. My heartbeat was pounding in my ears and I almost didn't hear the quietly spoken words.

"What?" I asked.

June parked the car and turned off the engine before turning to face me. She reached across the console and hesitantly grabbed my fists, gently coaxing them to loosen and rest in her hands. When her eyes met mine, I was surprised by the depth of pain and self-loathing reflected in them. Then she spoke and my breath caught in my throat.

"Eliza, you didn't do anything. Believe me when I tell you that none of this is your fault. If it's anyone's fault, then blame it on me. Take all your anger and pain out on me because nothing you do to me could hurt more than what I've done to you time and time again. Hate me, but please, I beg you, don't hate yourself. You are truly a beautiful soul that doesn't deserve the fate on your shoulders. But I can't stop it. It's too powerful. I've tried and have failed again and again, and I'm resigned to it because I don't know what else I can do. So please, Eliza, hate me, despise me, take all your pain out on me, because that is all I can offer you."

I had gained control over my breathing as I listened to June's words, but by the end, I felt another dam burst inside of me and I lunged across the console, dragging the surprised woman into a bone-crushing hug.

I held her for all I was worth, because while she was speaking, I had once again been filled with a sense of déjà vu that was quickly filled by a deeply rooted anguish from within that burst at the completely defeated look she gave me. I cried even as I remembered the strange dream I'd had last night and I imagined that the look she was giving me now must have been the look she would have been giving my dream self. She looked so lost.

I smothered my tears into her shoulder for what felt like hours. I could feel her holding me just as tightly and cooing softly in my ears, telling me over and over that it wasn't my fault and apologizing repeatedly. I slowly calmed down and released my death grip from around her neck. When I pulled back, she was smiling sadly. Embarrassed, I wiped the tears from my eyes and looked around as I felt the heat of a blush staining my cheeks. Looking out the passenger window, I realized we were parked in the lot behind my apartment building.

"I'm home."

"Yeah."

I turned back to her. "Will you come up with me?" I asked nervously.

She nodded. "If you need me to."

"I do."

"Then I'll come up for a while."

"Thank you."

"Don't thank me, Eliza. Please, don't ever thank me for offering you whatever small comforts I can."

I shook my head and gripped her hand tightly.

"Thank you, June. I feel like those are words I have told you many times and I don't plan on stopping now."

A pained look crossed her features, but she quickly hid it behind a small smile. "If that offers you comfort, then do so for your own benefit, but I am unworthy of your thanks."

"Then I'll keep saying it until the day you accept my words for what they truly are."

"And what is that?"

"An olive branch."

Shock lit up her subtle features, and I gripped her hands tighter and smiled.

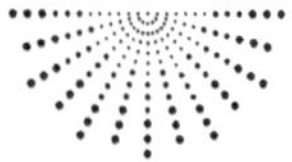

CHAPTER SIX

"Oh, do you want your jacket back?" I asked as I shut the door to my apartment behind us. June glanced at me, a small smile on her lips.

"Keep it."

"Are you sure?"

She nodded. "It looks good on you."

I blushed. "Thanks. It has grown on me."

I followed her into my living room and took a seat on the couch while June sat in the chair across from me. The sense of déjà vu flashed through me as I remembered how we were sitting like this only a little over a month ago.

"June—"

"Eliza—"

We called out at the same time.

"You go first—"

"Go ahead—"

I paused. June smiled. "I'm sure you've been dying to ask me some questions since our last meeting. So, you go first."

I nodded. "Okay, where did your mask go?"

She had the audacity to laugh at me.

"It's a legitimate question!"

"I know, it's just that out of all that you could have asked me, you chose to start there. You always start there. It's comforting."

I frowned at her comment but filed the questions it brought forth away for later.

"I guess to answer your asked question, my mask is inside me. It's as much a part of my body as my skin is, but that's not what you really wanted to ask. What you really want to know is what I am, but you're too polite to ask that question point-blank."

I frowned. For someone I've only spent less than an hour with, she knew me a little too well for comfort. "It's kind of rude just to ask someone what they are."

June nodded. "I'm a bone walker."

I paused. "What does that entail exactly?"

She frowned. "That's a little harder to answer in detail, but the simple answer is that we relocate souls."

"Relocate?"

"Some refer to it as reincarnation."

I paused.

"So, you're like the Grim Reaper?"

June looked thoughtful. "I guess in the sense that we take souls from the dead; but usually, the Grim Reaper is known to take souls to the afterlife. I don't do that; I recycle the souls that I take."

"Where do you take them?"

"My skill set allows me to transfer the souls I've collected into the developing bodies of a fetus during pregnancy."

"I see."

She sighed and sat up straighter. "Eliza, I'm not crazy."

When I didn't immediately agree with her, she sat up even straighter and a look of deep concentration settled on her features. I gasped as a fog rose around her face from seemingly nowhere, only to suddenly solidify and transform into the skull mask I had first laid eyes on.

"That could be special effects or something," I muttered, even as fear began to claw at my chest.

With the mask hiding her features I had to focus on her eyes to gauge her emotions, and all I could see in them was a patient tenderness.

"Eliza, this is your apartment."

"But you've been here before." Hysteria was beginning to enter my words as my grasp on reality began to slip. I don't know why I was reacting so badly. I think it's because on some level, I had been in denial about the whole thing. That somehow, I imagined the skull mask in my state of shock. But now that I was faced with it, it suddenly became too real. The supernatural world was slapping me in the face and I just wanted to turn the other cheek and pretend that the first slap never happened.

I watched in rapt fascination as the mask seemed to melt back into her face, revealing her angular features with bunched brows and downturned lips.

"I know this isn't easy, Eliza, but I need you to calm down." She spoke softly, as if she was talking me back from the ledge of a building—and I guess in some ways, she was.

I looked down and saw that my hands were gripping my leather jacket tight enough to make my knuckles white. I took several deep breaths and consciously relaxed my hands. I met June's gaze and could feel tears streaming down my face again as I stared helplessly into her eyes. Their unique color only added to the haunted look that seemed to be a constant in her gaze. They say that the eyes are windows to the soul. I could see that her soul was old, and maybe even as tormented as my own.

"Jeez, I never knew I was such a crybaby." I laughed and attempted to wipe the tears away before they fell.

"Why is this happening to me, June? Why?"

She was around the coffee table in seconds and wrapping her arms around me, pulling me into her chest.

"Shush, baby. It's okay. We don't have to deal with it anymore right now if you don't want to."

My heart fluttered at the term of endearment, and I had the vague sense of her having said something similar to me long ago. Once I gained control of my waterworks, I pulled back from her shoulder and placed my hand on her face, drawing her gaze to my own.

"I know you, June."

She frowned before nodding. "Yes, we met last month."

I shook my head. "No, June. I know you. I've known you for a long time; or at least, I feel like I do. Ever since you rescued me that day, I keep having these moments of déjà vu, from things you say or do. You said you recycled souls. Did you recycle mine?"

For a moment she simply gazed at me, blank-faced. Then, several emotions played out on her face, the most prominent being fear, but there was another. I couldn't immediately identify it before I was moved off her lap and back onto the couch. June was pacing back and forth, burning a hole in my living room rug while muttering to herself.

"When you said that earlier, I thought I misheard you. This has never happened before. All the other times your memory was completely wiped. How is this possible? It's not possible. It can't be."

Suddenly, she stopped and was grasping my shoulders. I could feel her hands trembling as she gazed at me intently and I was finally able to identify the emotion I had seen earlier on her face. The emotion had been a flicker of hope.

"Tell me everything you remember," she begged, and I nodded.

"Sorry…I…I didn't mean to scare you…" June trailed off as she pulled her hands back and stood up straight. "I just…"

She let out a sigh and walked over to the armchair across from me before dropping limply into it.

"Are you okay, June?" I whispered. "Is it that big of a deal that I remembered some things?"

Her head shot up from where she had been resting it in her hands. "So, you do remember? An entire memory of something that happened in another life? Not just fragments?"

I nodded. "I think so. It was a dream I had about a week ago. I don't remember the entire dream, but I do remember enough."

"How do you know it was a memory?"

"Well, because you were in it." I blushed as I remembered the warmth of her arms as they wrapped around me in the dream.

"I was?" She seemed at a loss for words, so I simply nodded.

"Plus, I've been having moments of déjà vu ever since that morning we met." I tried to suppress the other memories that came from that day even as I spoke.

"What happened in the dream?"

I blushed again. "Um…"

"Please, Eliza. I need to know. To make sure."

Her eyes held a desperation that I couldn't deny for the sake of my modesty, so I nodded. "Okay."

She seemed to sag with relief.

"Where should I start?"

"From where the dream began," she replied.

"Okay. Well, I was sitting on a beach, and I was dressed in

simple clothes, but I mostly remember that I was covered with all kinds of jewelry. You were sitting next to me, and we spoke for a while and then…" I trailed off.

"Then?"

"I think…"

"What?"

"Well, I think I died. It was just as the sun was beginning to rise. I think we were waiting for me to die. I don't know. It was a strange dream, and I'm not even sure if it was a memory. I just thought—"

"It is a memory." June cut me off.

"It is?"

"Yes." She sagged even deeper into the chair and dropped her head into her hands.

"It's just as she said. I didn't believe her. I wanted to, but I didn't think it was possible, but here is the proof. I can't deny it." I think she was speaking to herself, as I didn't understand a word she was saying.

"Who said what?"

June's head shot up. "Three thousand years."

"What?" I frowned.

"I've waited…we've been stuck in an endless cycle for three thousand years. Three hundred years ago, I met a woman. You would call her a psychic in this realm, but in my realm, we know of her as a Fate. Not *The* Fate, but one of her sisters. She told me…"

"What, June? What did she tell you?"

She seemed to take a deep breath, as if to steel herself for what she was about to say. "She told me that we would be given one chance—and only one—to break the cycle after three millennia of our curse had been served; but I didn't believe it was possible. Yet here you are. You remember things from your past life. That memory was from your life as an Egyptian princess. We were on the beach in Sharm el-

Sheikh. That took place in 332 BC, just before the invasion of Alexander the Great. He was the result of the side you chose that time."

"I chose the demons' side, right?"

June froze for a moment before speaking very quietly. "You remember which side you picked? You remember…"

I nodded hesitantly. "In my dream, I thought about the side I'd decided to pick. I don't understand exactly what that means, but you said it caused Alexander the Great to invade Egypt, so I'm assuming it wasn't something good."

She shook her head. "You are beyond good and evil."

I frowned. "No one is above good and evil."

"You are, Eliza. Only you are."

"Does this have to do with me choosing a side? Is the other side the angels' side or something?"

She hesitated. "I don't know how much I can tell you. I don't…this has never happened before. I'm not prepared. What should we do?" She seemed to be working herself into an endless loop of nerves. I reached out across the coffee table and took both of her hands into mine. She stopped talking.

"How about you take a deep breath first."

She nodded and breathed. "Sorry."

I shook my head. "It's fine. Now, let's talk."

"About what, exactly?"

"About the past, first. I need context before I can help."

"Help?" June furrowed her brow in that adorable puppy-like look that I was beginning to love.

"Yes, June. We will do this together."

"Together?" she parroted.

"This is our one chance, right? Well, I might not completely understand the situation, but I do know that you have been shouldering this burden by yourself for a long time. This time, though, I'm here for you. I can help. So I'm going to do everything in my power to fix this. Whatever this is. Do you understand?"

She stared at me blankly for a moment before a beautiful smile graced her lips. It was small but charming, nonetheless. It brought a smile to my own face because of the raw joy I found unveiled in her eyes. It dwarfed the usual pained look I had associated with her gray eyes and filled it to the brim.

"Okay." She nodded and tightened her hold on my hands.

"Good. I didn't want to have to beat you into submission."

She chuckled. "You could have tried, but I don't think you have enough muscle to beat me."

I tapped my head. "Who said anything about muscle? I have a sharp mind, which I've used to negotiate hard-to-get contracts with elusive companies. I have the mind of a sales-woman, and I would have found a way to bring you to my side."

June's smile spread just a little bit wider as she reached up to cup my face.

"All you would have to do is ask, Eliza. I would do anything to make you happy."

I felt the heat of a blush stain my cheeks even as I nodded. "I know. Help me understand why I know that."

She pulled her hand away and placed it back in my grasp. "Where should I start?"

"How about you begin with when this cycle was started. The how and the why. Then we will move forward from there."

"Okay, but let me warn you, it was a very long time ago."

"I'm sure I can handle it," I smirked.

"I'm sure you can."

"We will face this together, June," I said.

"I like the sound of that." Her eyes twinkled with an honest happiness I believed had been absent from them for a long time. Hope shone strongly in her gunmetal gray, and I'm sure it was reflected in my own.

I STUDIED THE WOMAN IN FRONT OF ME AS SHE COLLECTED HER thoughts. Finally, she met my gaze.

"Eliza—"

The sound of a ringtone blared out in the quiet of my living room, disrupting our conversation.

"Shit! Hold on. I have to take this." She pulled a flip phone from her jean pocket. It was black, with small skull stickers decorating it. I giggled.

"Don't ask," she muttered, and stood.

She went into the kitchen, and even though I could hear her speaking softly, I couldn't make out what she was saying. I looked around my living room. Was this really happening? This could all just be an elaborate dream.

"Understood. I'm on my way, sir." June's usually soft voice had a hard edge to it as she flipped her phone closed and walked back into the living room.

"Do you have to leave?"

"I'm sorry, Eliza. I know I said I would explain everything, but I have to go. It's important."

I nodded. "It's fine. I'm probably not the only person you have to watch over, or whatever it is your job demands."

June sighed and gave me a small smile. "Believe me when I say that you're the most important, but you're right. Duty calls, and when my boss calls me in I have to go, or else."

"Really, June. I don't mind. It's getting late, anyway. I think I'll order something, then go to bed."

She studied me for a moment before nodding. "I promise to explain everything next time."

I smiled. "I'll hold you to it."

June stood in place awkwardly, as if she was debating what to do next, then she came over to me and bent down. My heart quickened as her face neared mine and I thought for a moment she was going to kiss me and honestly, I don't think I would have minded. Instead, she pulled me into a quick hug, her scent surrounding me—along with the powerful emotions her proximity caused—then she pulled back.

"I'll come to you. Please, try and stay out of trouble. You tend to be a magnet for it. Oh, and, Eliza, you can't tell anyone about me or your memories. No one can know that things are different this time."

I nodded. "I think I can manage all of that. I've survived for twenty-five years on my own; one day won't do me in."

She frowned a moment, then walked the short distance to my front door and opened it. Hesitating, she turned back once more. "Please, promise me, Eliza."

I chuckled. "I promise I won't do anything stupid while you're gone."

She nodded, satisfied with that.

"Goodbye, June." I walked over and slowly began closing the door.

"Bye." She turned and took a few steps, only to suddenly flicker out of existence. I threw open my door and glanced around the hallway. She was gone. Completely gone. In the blink of an eye, she just disappeared into thin air, like some kind of magician.

"Shit," I whispered, and closed the door.

My apartment felt empty all of a sudden; cold. I went back into my living room and found my purse on the coffee table. I dug out my cell phone, a smartphone, unlike June's flip phone; I giggled at the thought. Pulling out a credit card, I located the Chinese menu that had been stuffed in my junk drawer in the kitchen and dialed the number from speed dial.

"Hello? Yes, I'd like delivery. Yeah, I want a large chicken lo mein with an extra egg roll." I thought for a moment, then ordered a sesame chicken just for the hell of it. My life was pretty weird right now. It wouldn't hurt to have a little extra in my belly.

I WOKE, DESPERATE FOR WATER. RUNNING TO THE KITCHEN, I filled a glass from the tap before guzzling it down in a few gulps. I gasped, then poured another one, drinking it a bit slower.

"Way too much MSG at that place," I muttered, and pulled two aspirin from the pill drawer. Being dehydrated always gave me a headache. I finished off the water with my pills and poured another glass, taking it into my living room where I plopped down onto the couch. As I nursed the water, the events of yesterday came back to me. Had that all been a dream? I shook my head. I just needed something to bring me back to reality. I picked my cell phone up off the coffee table where I'd placed it while I had chomped down on Chinese during my chick-flick marathon. Then I dialed one of the only saved numbers on my contacts list that wasn't a takeout place or an old coworker. It only rang once before a groggy voice answered.

"Yes?"

"Hey, Angela!" I chirped, only because I knew it would annoy her.

"Eliza! What do you want?" she groaned.

"Do you want to get breakfast?"

There was some shuffling on the other side of the line

followed by a loud yawn. "Sure. Let me just make myself presentable for the day."

I smiled. "Late night?"

She chuckled. "You could say that. I'll tell you about it once I've had my daily dose of caffeine. Where do you want to meet?"

"How about the usual?"

"Okay, just give me, like, thirty minutes."

"Sounds good. See you soon. And don't you dare fall back asleep!"

"Yes, mom."

"Damn straight."

Her laugh was cut off by the line cutting out. I smirked and stood. I needed to get ready if I was going to be on time, and I was sure that my hair was still a bird's nest. I groaned. Half an hour was never enough time.

Bear's was a hidden gem in Belltown. They did breakfast, lunch, and dinner, and were open twenty-four/seven, making them popular with the after-hours kind of crowd. It was also a frequent stop after barhopping all night. I'm sure they had the taxi service on speed dial and a deal worked out to benefit both parties. Angela and I have had a love affair with the place ever since they introduced their pride and joy, La Chupacabra. La Chupacabra was a breakfast burrito to rule all breakfast burritos. At a length of seven inches, it was a heart attack packed snuggly in a deceiving flour tortilla. It contained scrambled eggs, two fried eggs, three kinds of cheese (customer's choice), steak, bacon, fried potatoes, sour cream, and salsa, with guacamole on the side for an extra fifty cents. It was a personal challenge to one day eat the whole thing in one sitting. It was on my bucket list.

Bear's was close enough to my apartment that I could walk, which was great since I still wasn't ready to attempt the bus just yet and the train was out of the way. An hour later, I was sipping from a mug of coffee. I had asked the waiter to hold off on bringing out my order until Angela showed up, but I had already placed it, knowing she would just copy whatever I got.

I jerked when I felt a pair of cold hands cover my eyes. I was glad I didn't scream. It meant that I might finally be getting over the event from a month ago.

"Guess who?"

"You're late, and your hands are freezing! They're burning my eyeballs." I laughed as Angela removed her hands and sat across from me.

"You're grumpy this morning," she pouted.

"No, your hands were just blocks of ice. The temperature must have dropped since I came here."

She nodded as the waiter came over to take her order.

"I want what she's having, please."

"A coffee and the breakfast burrito?" he confirmed.

Angela smiled. "Yep, that sounds right."

The waiter nodded and scribbled it down on his notepad. "Be right out."

"Thank you."

He smiled. "No problem. I'll just get your coffee. Two creams and two sugars?"

"Yeah, sounds wonderful."

After he left, my friend began stripping off her winter gear. First, her beanie came off—it was decorated with snowflakes in a variety of colors—then her scarf and thermal-lined coat came off.

"You look like it was freezing outside."

She leveled me with a look. "Honey, there were flurries when I left my apartment. This getup was a necessity. You're going to freeze on your way home. You might want to take a taxi or the bus. I didn't drive, or I'd offer you a ride."

I shuddered at the mention of public transportation but

played it off with a shrug. "I think I'll stick with walking. It will be good for my allergies."

She looked at me strangely before shrugging. She had just opened her mouth when the waiter came back and set down a steaming mug.

"Thanks, you're a lifesaver."

He chuckled. "No problem. Your orders should be out soon. Can I get you anything else?"

I shook my head. "No thanks."

"Okay, well, enjoy." He walked off to help another table.

Angela moaned and wiggled her butt in her chair as she sipped her coffee. I snorted.

"If you love it so much, why don't you marry it?"

"I tried, but he keeps disappearing every morning. Mr. Coffee is an elusive lover. One moment, he's whispering sweet nothings to you, the next he's in someone else's kitchen giving them the time of their life. Just when you think you've tied him down..." She sighed wistfully and took another sip.

"You're so weird, Angela."

"That's why you love me. You get my personal brand of crazy."

I nodded. "And you get mine, I suppose."

"That's right. Now, tell me why you suddenly called me out for breakfast. Not that I'm not happy to be spending time with you; believe me when I say that it's been way too long since we just hung out. But you sounded stressed over the phone."

I took a sip of my now cooling coffee to collect my thoughts. "Is it possible to be in a waking dream and not know it?"

She frowned. "You mean like something from *Inception*?"

I thought about the movie and nodded. "Just like that."

"Why? Are you having nightmares again?"

I shook my head. "Not exactly."

Angela set her mug down and studied me for a moment before leaning forward and whispering, "Does this have to do with being attacked? Are you sure you're okay?"

I was touched by her concern, and I wanted to tell her everything that had happened. Even if she didn't understand, Angela always had a way of making me feel better about the worst situations. Just like how she helped me through the death of my foster mother during college. My best friend always knew what to say or do.

As I opened my mouth to tell her, June's voice entered my mind, *"You can't tell anyone about me or your memories. No one can know that things are different this time..."*

But surely, I could tell Angela, right? Besides, it was all a dream. Dreams can't hurt people, right? But what if it wasn't all a dream? What if it was all real? Could it hurt her then?

I felt a now warm hand gently squeeze my arm, bringing me from my thoughts. I looked up into Angela's worried gaze. "Are you okay, Eliza? Did someone try to hurt you again? Are you sure you don't want to stay at my place? You don't seem yourself."

The concern in her gaze assured me that I could tell her anything and it would work out. I opened my mouth. "Angela—"

"Eliza, what a coincidence it is meeting you here," a voice as smooth as silk cut me off, making my heart leap into my throat in the process. I looked up into the dark gaze of Kaleb.

"Kaleb? What are you doing here?" I all but yelled, still trying to calm down.

He looked around before meeting my gaze. "Apparently, I'm getting breakfast. I assume you are doing the same?"

I flushed at his words and was about to say something equally stupid when I was reminded of my company by the clearing of a feminine throat. We both looked at Angela, who was all but glowing in attraction to the overly handsome man next to me. The same man that had admitted to being a demon only a week ago. That is, if I wasn't losing my mind and hadn't imagined the entire thing. I had to get him away from her either way.

"Who's your friend, Eliza?"

I frowned. He sounded way too interested to be a good thing.

"Angela, meet Kaleb. I met him at my art show."

He received her hand, kissing her knuckle before smirking in all his deadly glory. "Pleasure. Kaleb Cole, at your service."

"Aren't you cute?" she giggled. My frown deepened. Angela only giggled when she was flirting. This wasn't going well. I needed to get him away from her.

"Are you eating with anyone, Kaleb?" she asked.

He pouted and shrugged. "Sadly, it seems I was stood up by my date. I was just on my way out when I spotted a familiar face."

Angela tried to hide her glee at hearing this but it was a waste of time. I internally groaned, as I knew what was coming next.

"Why don't you join us then? We don't mind, right, Eliza?"

I stood as I noticed our waiter coming over with our food. Finally, my luck was working for once. "Actually, I have to go."

She frowned. "Don't be silly, we just got here."

"You mean, *you* just got here. I've been waiting here for a while, and now I'm leaving." I felt a pang of guilt as I watched her face fall. I hated doing this, but I hated the idea of Kaleb being around my best friend more. Especially if he was, in fact, a demon. God, I was going crazy.

"Oh, sorry about that," she muttered.

I turned to the confused waiter. "Can you please put one of those in a to-go box?"

"Um, sure," he said, and placed one of the plates down on the table in front of Angela, then walked off.

We waited in an awkward silence for the moment it took the waiter. I shuffled from foot to foot. The restaurant was bustling with life and sounds from people enjoying meals with loved ones. As an observer, their lives all seemed so uncomplicated, while mine felt like it was spiraling out of control. If that wasn't a depressing thought, to top it all off, I might be losing my mind.

"Here's your box, miss."

I jerked a little, but quickly recovered and took the offered box. I turned and slapped a twenty on the table, startling Angela in the process. She had been picking at her food. "I'll call you," I said, then grabbed Kaleb's hand, dragging him away from one of the only people that mattered in my life. He let me pull him all the way out of the restaurant before I released him. When I turned around, he was smirking.

"What?" I snapped.

He shrugged. "I didn't say anything."

"You might as well have!" I yelled, then turned to walk away but was stopped by a hot hand on my shoulder. I turned back to him.

"Why don't I walk you home? It's dangerous around here."

"I can take care of myself."

"Are you sure?"

"I think I would know."

"Maybe Angela would like some company then. I'm sure she's a bit lonely after her best friend so rudely left her on her own." He turned to go back into Bear's, but I grabbed his hand.

"Fine, you bastard. Walk me home."

"My pleasure," he chuckled, and pulled my arm through his, wrapping them around one another and pulling me snuggly into his side.

"You're an asshole."

"Only when it suits me."

We began walking in the direction of my apartment, with him leading. I don't know what concerned me more. The fact that he knew where I lived or that I was alone with a man that could possibly be a demon.

"No need to be so tense. I promise, I don't bite."

"How can I be sure?"

He held his hand over his heart. "Scout's honor."

"Do you even have a heart?"

He simply smirked. "Smart girl."

"Shut up."

"I assure you that I mean you no harm. It wouldn't suit my purpose."

"And what exactly is that?"

His eyebrows went up. "Don't you know?"

I frowned. "Should I?"

"I guess it's against the rules for her to tell you much. Makes sense," he mused.

"Are you going to tell me or just leave me in the dark?"

"The dark is exactly where I want you, my dear." He grinned, and for a moment, the light around us shifted just right and the man holding my arm in his grasp wasn't a man at all. He was a grotesque creature. He defied all logic with his disfigurements: horns curved like a ram's, blood-red eyes that looked hungry, teeth jagged and sharp like a shark's, and skin like smoked stone. The scent of smoke surrounded me and it made my eyes water. Then, like a mirage in the desert, he was back to normal. A good-looking man. I jerked my hand from his grasp and trembled. I suddenly felt tired, weak. I sighed. "What do you want from me, Kaleb?"

"What we all want from you."

I met his dark gaze. "And what is that?"

"For you to make a choice that will benefit us. That is all, Eliza. We just want you to choose."

I looked around and was surprised to see we were in front of my apartment building. I turned back to him. "Why?"

"Because, my girl, it is why you were born. Your pain is my pleasure; your suffering is my nectar. I stand for all of your hate and anger; the hate and pain gathered from lifetimes of injustice. I offer you the power to take your revenge against the light. All you have to do is choose me."

I shook my head. "Not today, Kaleb. I won't make a choice today. Leave me now. Your smell is making me sick."

He chuckled. "My apologies, Ms. Trust. The smell of a demon can overwhelm a mere mortal. I'll have to keep that in mind when I'm around you."

"Or you could just stay away from me."

He shook his head. "Where would the fun be in that?"

I nodded. "Leave me now. I want to be alone."

"As you wish." He gave a low, sweeping bow before continuing on his way. I watched until he rounded the corner and was out of sight before I walked inside to escape the chill that had settled deep within my bones. It had been warm in his presence. Maybe that had to do with his being a demon. Either way, I was now freezing, so I quickly entered the elevator. I just wanted to go back home and climb into my warm bed.

"Why?" I whispered into the silence of the hallway as the elevator closed, shutting out the chill of fall.

CHAPTER SEVEN

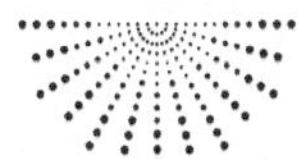

I was chopping carrots for the chicken noodle soup I was attempting to make for dinner when there was a loud thumping at my front door.

"Who could that be?" I wondered and left my carrots, which looked more like hamster food because I was never good at chopping—or cooking in general, for that matter. Angela was always trying to teach me a few things, but they never seemed to stick. I paused while unlocking the door, my hand hanging awkwardly in the air. What if it was Angela? I didn't know if I was ready to face her just yet. The peephole in my door had been busted before I rented the apartment. The landlord hadn't been too forthcoming with the details of how it happened; I had my suspicions that either an angry boyfriend or girlfriend was involved, but I had managed to get a little bit off my rent because of it, and I had the repairman fill it with plaster. Now, I was regretting that decision.

I huffed. "What's the worst that can happen?"

Then, I opened the door. A body all but fell on top of me, causing me to yelp. "What the—"

I caught the body and stumbled a little, only to see the white-gold strands of hair that only belonged to one person I knew. "June?"

She stepped back, and I gasped. She was deathly pale, but there was an unhealthy blush on her cheeks that suggested either she was drunk, or running a high fever. Her usually soft voice sounded hoarse as it disrupted me from my thoughts. "Sorry, I tripped."

"Are you okay? Come on in and sit down."

She stumbled a little and I grabbed her by her shoulders to help steady her. She let out a pained gasp.

"What? Is something wrong with your back?"

"It's nothing," she whispered as she let me lead her into my living room, closing the door behind us.

"You look horrible."

"It's nothing, really. I'd like to stand if you don't mind."

She resisted with surprising strength when I tried to push her down onto the couch.

"June, what's wrong with you?"

"I'm fine—" She yelped when I slapped her on the back.

"Uh huh, I'm sure you are," I said as I drew off her leather jacket. It was a new one; probably a replacement for the one she gave me. It was a nice caramel color that went well with her hair.

"Eliza, you don't need—"

"Lift your arms."

She sighed and attempted to do as I instructed. She was wearing a black shirt, but it felt wet, and my concern grew as I slowly lifted it around her head. I gasped. Nothing could have prepared me for the sight of her back. It was a ripped and bloody mess.

"What the fuck, June?"

"Don't, Eliza," she warned.

"Don't fucking what? Worry about you? You know what?

Don't answer that. Stay here!" I yelled, and left her to get the first aid kit that I kept in my kitchen for cooking mishaps. I came back quickly and she was right where I left her, gripping her jacket to her chest. She looked over her shoulder. "Eliza, don't look at me like that. I'm—"

I held up my hand. "Don't finish that sentence. I'll lose it if you do. Just...just let me help you. Please. I...I need to do something."

She nodded.

"Can you lay down on the couch? You're too tall. It will be easier for me to treat you."

She walked over and lay down on her stomach.

"Thank you," I whispered as I set to work.

I had to stop several times to take a deep breath and still my shaking hands. I did the best I could to wipe off the blood and clean the wounds of dirt, but there honestly wasn't much I could do. June told me it wouldn't help to wrap it. She instructed me to just clean it with alcohol and let it air dry. It didn't feel like enough. Nothing I did ever felt like enough. I wanted to cry, to relieve some of the frustration, but my eyes were dry. Even my own body was rebelling against me.

I finished and surveyed the damage. There were raised welts as well as long slashes, as if nails had dug in and dragged along her back. It was going to scar, I thought absently, and cleaned up my mess. Thankfully, it wasn't bleeding anymore, but her back looked like she had been put through the shredder.

I stood from my kneeling position and winced as my knees cracked. My legs had fallen asleep. I looked down at the woman on the couch. She had fallen asleep too. How she did with the pain she must have been in was a mystery to me, but it was probably for the best. People healed better when they were sleeping.

I went back into the kitchen, setting the first aid kit down on the table, and turned around only to stop when I noticed the chopped carrots. A thought came to my mind as I gazed at the small pieces of orange that were too small for their purpose; I hadn't chopped the carrots. I had diced them.

Bursting into tears, I wailed, "I can't even chop carrots properly!" I gasped in between sobs as they racked my body. Sinking into the chair at the table, I laughed and cried until my belly hurt and my eyes were sore. Then I poured a glass of water and took two aspirin. I grabbed the whole bottle of pills and poured another glass of water, taking both into the living room, and set them down on the coffee table. She would need them in the morning. I took a seat in the armchair across from June.

Our position had been reversed. It wasn't that long ago, but it felt like years now, when in fact it had only been a little over a month since the first time she saved me. I pushed the thoughts from my mind. I could think about it tomorrow. I glanced up at the cheap plastic clock, a Walmart special, hanging on the wall above my television. Ten o'clock. A little early, but I was beyond exhausted. I don't think I'd ever had such an eventful week. I pulled the blanket off the back of the chair and wrapped it around myself. It would be best to leave June uncovered. A sheet might irritate her wounds. Snuggling down, I drifted off into a dreamless sleep.

***

"GET SOME BITCHES!" I JERKED AWAKE AND LOOKED AROUND IN confusion.

"I said, get some bitches and some cha-ching."

"Shit!" I jumped up, throwing off the blanket in my mad dash to get to the kitchen where my purse was. Digging through it, I pulled out my cell phone. I already knew who was calling by the ringtone that she had put on my phone without my knowledge. She was always changing it every time I slept over at her place after a drinking binge.

"Hello?"

"What the hell was that yesterday at breakfast?"

"Shit, Angela. I'm sorry."

"Yeah, you better be. If you didn't want to hang out with me, you could have just told me you were feeling sick."

"What?" Now I was confused.

"I get that you were sick. You should have just said so."

"No, Angela. I just didn't want to talk to Kaleb. He's not that great of a guy."

"What are you talking about, Eliza?"

I frowned. "Kaleb? The guy that showed up. I don't like him. I didn't want you to meet him."

"Who is Kaleb? I'm talking about how you puked all over the waiter when he brought out our order. You didn't have to force yourself to go out with me if you were that sick. I wouldn't have been angry if you'd canceled. Are you feeling better now?"

I trembled. Was I losing my fucking mind? The feeling of reality shifting once more filled me with dread even as I went into the living room. A chill ran down my spine when I walked to stand over June.

"Shit. Yeah, I'm fine, Angela. I have to go. I'll call you some other time." I hung up without waiting for a response. I studied June's back with trepidation. It was smooth, pale skin. There were no scars, or tears, or blemishes. Just perfect skin.

"Shit!" I yelled in disbelief.

June jerked awake and rolled. I moved back, and she yelped when she hit the floor. She scrambled for a moment and looked around in confusion. It would have been funny if I wasn't freaking out. She looked up at me, frowning. "Eliza? Are you okay?"

"You're not real," I whispered.

"What did you say? I couldn't hear you." She stood, grabbing her shirt off the coffee table. She grimaced at it before shrugging and putting it on.

"I said you're not fucking real!"

She frowned. "What are you talking about?"

"It's finally happened. I've lost it. I've lost my mind." I was pacing while babbling.

"Eliza!"

I didn't stop. "I'm bonkers!"

"Eliza!"

"The cuckoo has flown the coop!"

"Eliza!" She grabbed my arm and I whirled on her.

"You!"

She looked taken aback. Good. "What?"

"This is all your fault."

"It is?"

"You and your hockey mask! You've made me insane with your talk of past lives and stuff. You don't even exist!"

Her brows furrowed. "Don't be ridiculous, Eliza."

"You're the ridiculous one. You're worse than an imaginary friend."

"Eliza!"

"No, stop talking. I don't want to hear it."

There was a knock at the front door. "I'll prove it to you!" I yelled as I walked down the hallway and threw open the door, revealing the startled and concerned face of my neighbor, Ms. Jean. She smiled hesitantly. "I heard yelling. Is everything all right?"

"Ms. Jean, this is going to sound strange, but can you see this woman standing next to me?"

Ms. Jean looked puzzled, but turned to look at June and smiled. "Of course, dear, I'm not that old yet. You're the woman that helped me carry my groceries to my apartment all those days ago. Thank you, by the way. I never caught your name?"

"My name is June, ma'am. There is no need to thank me. It was no problem."

Ms. Jean nodded. "Aren't you a sweetheart. Well, I see everything over here is fine. I've just finished my morning walk, so I'm going to go and make breakfast now. Take care, girls, and I'm sorry for intruding." My neighbor turned around and left as I slowly closed my front door.

"She...she saw you." I looked up and met June's gaze. "You're real."

She frowned. "Yes, Eliza. Of course I'm real."

"But Kaleb—"

"Kaleb is a demon. If he doesn't want people to remember him, they won't. What you did yesterday was dangerous. Do you understand that? You're lucky he didn't kidnap you. I wasn't there to oversee things. Anything could have happened. He could have taken you, and I might not have been able to find you—"

"June! I understand, calm down."

Her face was losing what little color she had managed to get back after a rest, and turning pale with each word she spoke as if she was the one realizing the severity of her own words. She took a deep breath. "I'm sorry. I just...I'm sorry."

"It's okay."

"No, it's not! I wasn't doing my job. I wasn't protecting you like I should have been!"

"You're right."

She paused. "I'm right?"

"Yeah. You were too busy having your back turned into shreds. What was that about anyway, huh? Did you get into a fight or something?"

June frowned. "That's not your concern."

"The hell it isn't! What happened after you left my apartment? Did it have to do with that phone call?"

Her face flushed. "You don't get to turn this on me! You're the one that went galivanting around with a demon yesterday! Why would you do that? Was he too handsome to resist, is that it? Have you chosen to go with his side already? After everything we've discussed?"

I watched as her face flushed bright red, starting from the tips of her ears and ending at her neck. I couldn't believe what I was hearing. I waited until she was done speaking before I answered.

"You're jealous."

She froze. "What?"

"I don't believe it, but you're jealous that I hung out with Kaleb."

June's brow furrowed. "Don't be ridiculous. Kaleb is dangerous—"

"You're turning green."

"That's not true! Stop saying that. I'm worried about you, that's all."

I stopped and studied the woman in front of me. She had an adorable pout on her face. I smiled. "I'm sorry, June."

She looked up.

"I'm sorry I was alone with Kaleb. It won't happen again."

She sighed. "Why would you let him walk you home anyway? You must have sensed the danger."

I studied my nails as I felt my face heat up. "I was in denial."

"Denial of what?"

I threw my arms up. "Of everything! All of this! Bone walkers, demons, and angels. It wasn't that long ago that this was the stuff of myths. Past lives, reincarnation, choosing sides. It's a little hard to take it all in, let alone believe it all."

"Is that why you asked your neighbor if she could see me?"

"I thought you were a figment of my imagination. I thought I was going crazy." I sighed.

June reached out and took my hands into hers. "I'm sorry, Eliza. I've been known to move too fast with these things. I take for granted that I've done this many times, but in this life, this is your first time learning about all of this. Will you forgive me?"

I shrugged. "It's fine. I'm sorry I freaked out."

June used her hand to tilt my jaw up so I would meet her gaze. "Together, right?"

I smiled. "Yeah."

She nodded. "Good."

I chuckled. "You were still totally jealous."

Her brows furrowed before smoothing her features into a smirk. "Can you really blame me? You're amazing. Anyone would have to be blind not to see that."

I blushed and smiled shyly. The fluttery feeling I always got around her intensified in my stomach along with the confusion the emotions always brought forth. I pushed it all to the back of my mind and cleared my throat. "Don't think you're going to get out of telling me why you were injured or how you healed so quickly."

She frowned. "It was nothing."

"June," I warned.

She sighed. "Fine. It was a punishment."

"Punishment? For what?"

"For interfering."

"With what?"

"With Gabriel's time."

"What are you—" I cut myself off as I remembered the altercation I'd had at the gallery.

"That asshole!"

"It's my fault, Eliza."

"The hell it is! I'll give him a piece of my mind—"

"You can't."

I turned to her. "Why not?"

"You can't do anything. You're not supposed to know anything about them until they reveal themselves to you. I wasn't supposed to tell you anything, and you're not supposed to remember anything from your past lives. You can't say anything."

I deflated. "But they hurt you because of me."

"It's fine, Eliza. It was my fault. I know the rules. And I broke them knowing the consequences of my actions. I don't regret it, so don't worry about it."

"I hate him." I could feel the truth of that statement even as I uttered the words. I also felt like it wasn't the first time I had said something similar.

June pulled me into her arms. "No, Eliza. I don't want that. I don't want you to take revenge for me. I never have and I never will. It will be different this time, remember? We are going to break the cycle. So, don't think like that, please."

I gripped her shirt tightly and nodded into the crook of her neck. "Fine; but how did you heal so quickly?"

"Call it a perk of my profession."

"Okay."

She rubbed her hand up and down my back. "Good. Everything will be all right. We will work this out."

Even as her words soothed my anger, I felt the coldness of fear grip me. "I'm scared, June. What if it doesn't work out? We only get one chance. What if we fail?"

She pulled back, cupping my cheek. "We won't."

"How can you be so sure?"

"Because, I won't let us fail."

"But you're just one person."

She shook her head. "No, Eliza. Together. We are in this

together. And that is all we need to succeed. It's different this time. We won't let ourselves fail."

I nodded as I became lost in her gaze. It was like looking into a foggy morning. I couldn't see where I was going, but I took comfort in knowing that parts of June would be revealed little by little as the fog lifted in layers. One day, all that would be left was the sun, and that emotion in the distance. An emotion I still didn't have a name for but was hidden deep within the fog. With time and patience, I was sure I would soon learn its name.

"Okay."

"Good girl." She smiled, and another layer of the fog in her gaze cleared, revealing a little bit of joy.

CHAPTER EIGHT

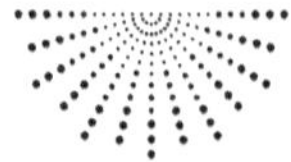

$\mathcal{I}$ held my Garfield mug containing the ambrosia of life, also known as coffee, while watching the woman at the other end of my kitchen table. June had helped me clean up the mess I left in my kitchen last night after another failed attempt at making soup.

"So, let me get this straight. You don't eat or drink anything?"

She smiled. "I tell you that I'm an eternal soul that is tasked with the job of reincarnation, among other things, and all you take away from that is that I don't require sustenance?"

I held up my hand. "Hold up. I'm still on the part where you said you don't eat or drink."

She chuckled.

"So, you're telling me that you've never had this life-giving drink?" I pointed to my mug.

June shook her head. "Coffee? No, I've never tried it; though it does smell nice."

"You've never had coffee? How have you survived this long without it?"

"I've managed."

"No! I won't believe it."

"What?"

"I accept that you're, like, an eternal soul and blah blah blah, but I refuse to accept that you've never had coffee. It wakes the dead, you know?" I said matter-of-factly.

She looked thoughtful. "Coffee has been around a long time, but it didn't exist before I became a bone walker."

I frowned. "How old are you?"

"I don't have an exact date, as we didn't keep track of it back then besides the rising and setting of the sun, but I think it's safe to say that I'm over three thousand years old."

I hummed and drank from my mug. "Okay, so you're a grandma. I can accept that. But even grandmas need coffee."

Her eyebrow ticked. "I'm not a grandma."

"Yes, you are."

"Don't call me that. It's weird."

"But you're, like, a really old lady."

"Technically, I'm not even alive."

"Okay, so a dead old lady; but you're still old."

She shook her head. "We're getting off topic."

I took another drink. "Fine, change the subject. I will never forget your imperfections."

June smiled. "As I was saying, bone walkers do Death's work—"

"What does he do if you do all his work?"

"He manages us."

"Like a boss?"

"Exactly, like a boss."

"What a lazy bastard."

She grinned. "I agree. Now, let me finish what I was saying."

"Continue." I waved my hand absently.

"Thanks. So, we do Death's work by collecting the souls of the dead."

"Where do you keep them?"

"What?"

"Where do you keep all the souls you take? Do you keep them on ice or something, until you pass them on?"

"On ice? No, we keep them in a layer of space we call our Pot of Souls."

"Oh. Then what do you do with them?"

"We hold onto them until we are given the order on where to place them."

"Where do you place them?"

"Inside the fetus of a pregnant woman."

I frowned. "You've said that before; but how exactly do you do that?"

"Through touch."

"Let me make sure I'm hearing this right. You're telling me that you make people pregnant by touching them?"

She laughed. "No! They are already pregnant. When we touch them, we can transfer the soul into their baby."

I nodded. "Okay, I was worried there for a second."

"You didn't need to be."

"Okay, so you're like Death's minion, and you go around popping souls into pregnant women's babies. Do you get paid or something? Eternal health insurance? Bonuses? Free pens? Anything?"

June stared at me for a moment. "No."

"No?"

"No, Eliza. No to all of that."

"That doesn't sound very fun."

"It's not supposed to be."

"So, why do you do it then? How does one become a bone walker?"

"They sign a contract with Death."

"A contract?"

"Yes."

"A minion contract."

She paused. "I guess you could call it that."

I nodded. "Okay."

"Okay?"

"Yeah, okay."

"That's all you have to say?"

I took a drink. "What do you want me to say?"

She frowned. "Okay. I guess."

"Well, that's what I said. So, we're good."

"Okay."

We paused. I burst out laughing.

"You look so confused." I tried to get control over my breathing.

"You are a very confusing woman."

"I'll take that as a compliment. I like to keep people on their toes."

"Well, you sure do that."

I snorted, then took another drink. The warm liquid warmed me in my freezing kitchen, reminding me that I hadn't paid my heating bill yet.

"So, how exactly do I play into all of this?" I placed my mug down. It was now empty. Standing, I motioned for her to follow me into the living room. "Let's talk in here. I'm getting cold."

"Oh, sorry. I don't feel the shift in temperatures."

"Lucky you."

"I guess. Do you want a blanket?"

"That would be nice." I smiled as she pulled one off of the armchair and handed it to me as I plopped down on the couch. "Thanks."

"No problem."

"Where was I?" I asked as I wrapped the blanket around

myself, cocooning into it.

June smiled before turning serious. "You play into it by making a choice."

"A choice? Between what?"

"Between sides."

"What sides?"

She didn't answer, but waited patiently. Then it clicked.

"I have to choose between the angels' or demons' side?"

She nodded and sat down next to me. "Yes, Eliza. Usually, that's what would happen. You would go through the negotiation period where a representative from each side would try to persuade you into choosing them."

"Gabriel or Kaleb?"

"Yes."

"What about you?"

She frowned. "I'm like a referee. I make sure they don't kill you before you make a choice."

"Why would they do that?" I felt a sudden chill that had nothing to do with the lack of heating.

"Well, they could just kill you and take your soul without letting you choose."

"But that's cheating, right?"

"Exactly; that's why I'm here. You're taking this all really well, by the way."

I shrugged. "I've freaked out and cried enough. I'm resigned to all of this supernatural stuff. Apparently, I've done it a million times already. Might as well get with the program, you know?"

She studied me.

"What."

"You never cease to amaze me."

I felt my face heat up as my eyes were drawn to her beautiful grays. I couldn't look away from the raw adoration I saw displayed in them. They were like deep pools of raging water.

I could drown in that water if I weren't careful. Maybe I *wanted* to drown in that water. It might not be so bad…and it couldn't be worse than my other options. I didn't know I had moved until June cleared her throat. My face was only inches away from hers. I jerked back and cleared my throat. My face was burning.

"So, uh, isn't the angels' side the good side? Why would I ever choose the demons' side?" I asked.

June shook her head. "I keep telling you, Eliza; you are outside the realm of good and evil."

"I just don't understand what that means."

June studied me for a moment before nodding. "It is indisputable that where there is light, there will also be shadow in its wake, right?"

I frowned. "I guess; but I don't see how that has anything to do with—"

She held up her hand. "Humor me."

I crossed my arms over my chest and huffed. "Fine."

"Just because it is light, would that mean it is, therefore, good, or holy in some way?"

"I guess not."

"Right, because light is just light, and shadow is just the absence of light. It is humans that assign a higher meaning to them, but the truth is that on a hot day everyone seeks the shade, and on a cool day, people turn their eyes to the sun."

I shook my head. "What exactly are you saying?"

"That good and evil are defined by human morals, but in the grand scheme of things, the bigger picture, good and evil don't exist. All that exists are events."

"Events?"

June nodded. "Angels represent morals, humans morals. They do their Master's bidding and their master sees the benefit of keeping humans alive."

"And what benefit is that, exactly?"

"Their master gains power from their prayers. The more people that pray to it, the stronger the master is, the better it can defend against the demons that seek to enter its realm."

I shook my head. "You lost me."

She frowned. "Events, Eliza. Depending on which side you choose, events are forced down the path of one of two possibilities."

"And they are?"

"Revenge, or morals."

"Not good or evil?"

June sighed. "You either choose the demons' side, and the scale is tipped toward revenge, which leads to destruction and chaos; or you choose the angels' side, and humans make advancements in medicine or soldiers unexpectedly come home from battle."

"That still sounds like either a good or bad outcome to me."

She shook her head. "If some soldiers come home from battle, that means others were deployed to replace them. And natural disasters, like forest fires or floods, with time, replenish the Earth in new ways. The ashes left behind by fire are fertile ground for new life to take root."

I uncrossed my arms. "I see. I would call those gray areas then."

June shrugged. "Call them what you will. We define them as events, since our jobs aren't really affected by either choice too much. Either way, people die, and souls are collected and relocated."

I nodded. "I think I'm beginning to understand. But I don't understand why I have to choose. Why do I exist?"

Pain entered her gaze. "Your job was created to keep the balance, after the fall of the Morning Star and the demons organized under their new master. Before that, demons had only been an annoyance at their worst. But with their organization, they became a terrible force and a threat. Death created the Lamb of Essence System in order to call a truce from the war. Both sides agreed, but they still needed a soul…" She trailed off.

"But why my soul? I'm no one—"

"It's my fault!" she cut in as her hands gripped into fists.

"How is it your fault?"

"Because…"

She remained silent.

"Why, June? You can tell me. I won't blame you," I whispered, taking one of her fists into my grasp. She mumbled.

"I didn't catch that."

June met my gaze, pulling her hand away. Her eyes were hard, empty. "Because I died."

I frowned. "What?"

June wouldn't meet my gaze as she spoke. "I died, Eliza, and Death tricked me. He made me sign the bone walker's contract, taking me out of the cycle of reincarnation without letting my soul choose a side."

"I don't understand, June."

She looked up, finally meeting my gaze. This time her gray gaze was a bottomless pit of self-loathing. "It doesn't matter. Only the truth matters, and the truth is that this is all my fault."

My mouth moved without conscious thought, and the words that escaped were both mine and not mine. "Then tell me a beautiful lie."

Her face froze in what could only have been shock. "What did you say?"

"The truth is an ugly lie. I want you to tell me a beautiful lie. Lie to me, June, because the truth has killed me over and over again, but your beautiful lies have given me life just as many times."

My heart was bursting with an emotion I hadn't felt in a

long time. I wasn't quite sure I remembered the name for it, but it had always filled me whenever I was around this woman. It was pure and powerful, and it was as heavy as it was light. Her hands trembled as they cupped my face. She wiped the tears that had fallen without my knowledge. Then she both sobbed and laughed as she gave me the name of the emotion. "I love you, Eliza Trust. I will always love you."

I gave her a watery smile. "You always were the best liar."

June crashed her mouth into mine. Our teeth bumped from the force behind it; the desperation. My arms wrapped around her neck, pulling her fully into me so I couldn't tell where she began and I ended. Her tongue ran along the seam of my lips and I gasped when she bit me, allowing her tongue to enter and explore; to claim what had never truly been hers.

I could taste both blood and the salt from my tears, but I only pulled myself more flush to her. This was the taste of hope, and it was glorious in its potency. It was the taste of pain—June's pain. Most of all, it was the taste of our ever-lasting love. Of all the lies that were truths in disguise, and it hurt so much as it settled in my chest, filling my heart to the brim.

I felt more tears slide down my face as our tongues met and slid gently against each other. I could feel her grip on my hair relax as she moaned. Our kiss began to slow, become more languid as the desperation settled down and the need for air became too demanding. We separated slowly, both panting.

June's gaze was soft as she studied my face like she was studying a great work of art. She whispered, "I've been waiting to do that for three millennia."

I smirked as I gasped out, "What took you so fucking long?"

She tipped her head back and let loose a laugh. It was

light and airy, soft and beautiful, but most of all it was hers, and I loved it just for that.

I smiled as I caught my breath. "I think I'm in love with you too, June."

She met my gaze and smiled.

"I just wanted you to know."

She nodded. "I do. I have. And I always will."

I WOKE FEELING A BIT SICK. I FELT LIKE THERE WAS COTTON IN my mouth, along with a faint throb in my head. As I climbed out of bed to get some aspirin, flashes of the night before entered my mind. June and I had spoken for a while longer, during which, I finally opened the bottle of Spanish red wine that had been collecting dust in my kitchen. I may have gotten a bit drunk. Okay, I got a lot drunk; but who would blame me? My life had suddenly become a drama, and I just needed a night to blow off some steam.

Around one in the morning, June had put me to bed, where I must have promptly passed out because I was drawing a blank after that. I groaned as I remembered trying to kiss her goodnight. It had been a sloppy attempt, but she had been a good sport about it and dodged like a pro.

I popped two pills into my mouth and washed them down with water as I went into my living room. Surprisingly, June was not sleeping on my couch. Actually, she wasn't anywhere in my apartment. Going back into my bedroom, I found a note on my bedside table. It simply stated that she was called into work for an emergency, and ended with a warning for me to stay out of trouble, followed by her cell phone number.

"How romantic," I sighed. She could have at least drawn a heart. It would have been better than nothing.

I walked over to my chest of drawers and pulled out a pair of skinny black jeans that were tastefully ripped at the knees and a long-sleeved white t-shirt with a frowny face printed on it. Grabbing underwear and socks, I hopped into the shower and set to scrubbing the stink of alcohol off. After mouth-washing twice and dressing, I was pouring my first cup of coffee when my phone rang. Pulling it from my purse, I saw the word *Philo's* on the caller ID.

"Shit!" I set my mug down and answered it.

"Hello, Eliza speaking," I said in my all-business tone.

"Ms. Trust? This is Jessica, Mr. Smead's assistant."

"Henry's assistant?" Was Smead his last name? I couldn't remember.

"That's correct. I'm calling to ask if you would be okay with having the meeting to sign your contract this afternoon. I know it's short notice, but Mr. Smead had a sudden cancellation and wanted to try and fit you in. I'm afraid this will be his only opening for a while. His schedule is packed with the holidays coming up. I'm sure you understand."

"Of course, but I'm afraid I haven't spoken with my lawyer yet. I thought I would have more time."

"Would it be possible to call him now? Mr. Smead is eager to sign you on as soon as possible."

"Let me call him now then. Can I reach you at this number?"

"Yes."

"Okay, I'll call you back as soon as I can. What time is the meeting?"

"Please be here at noon sharp."

"All right I'll see what I can do."

"Thank you, Ms. Trust. Once again, I'm sorry for the short notice."

"No problem. Let me make the call, then I'll get back to you."

"Of course. Bye."

"Bye."

I hung up, took a deep breath, and dialed my lawyer.

"Peter Roy's office, this is May speaking."

"May? This is Eliza Trust."

"Oh, Eliza! It's been a while. Happy holidays!"

"Back at you. Is Peter in?"

"He's on a coffee break, but he won't mind me putting you through."

"Thank you."

"No problem," she chirped.

Peter and I had gone to Washington University together. I wasn't originally as close with him as I was to Angela, but he and Angela had dated for a while. Once they broke up, he had tried to chase after me on the rebound, but I was never really interested. Instead, we became good friends. He was now happily married to May; going on five years now. May was a sweetheart, and sent me a card every Christmas. He couldn't have done better.

"Eliza?"

"Peter. How are you?"

"Fine, how about yourself?"

"I'm good."

"What can I do for you, Eliza?"

I took a deep breath. "I have a huge favor to ask of you."

"Oh? This is rare. Usually, I'm asking *you* for favors."

I laughed.

"What do you need?"

I cleared my throat. "The short story is that I need to sign a contract to show my art at a gallery. I'm trying to get into it."

"Congratulations, Eliza! I see Angela has had her way once again," he chuckled.

"Yeah."

"So, you need me to go over it with you?"

"Actually, I need you to meet me at the gallery for the signing."

"Okay, when is it?"

"Noon."

He was quiet. "Oh."

"I'm sorry, Peter. It's kind of an emergency or I wouldn't have thrown this on you."

"No, it's fine. I'll have May clear my schedule for this afternoon."

I sighed. "Thank you, Peter."

"It's not every day that you ask me for a favor. It sounds like you're doing well, though."

I thought about what this past month and a half had been like and nearly laughed. "You don't know the half of it."

"We'll have to talk over coffee sometime. May misses her tea dates with you and Angela."

I sighed at the memory of simpler times, and my eyes began to water. "Yeah, I miss them too, Peter. I miss them a lot."

"We'll just have to plan some more then." He chuckled. "So, where am I going this afternoon?"

I wiped my eyes. "Do you know where Philo's is?"

"The one in Queen Anne?"

"Yeah."

"Wow, you really have done well for yourself."

"I try."

"Okay, I'll tell May, and I'll see you there."

"Thanks again, Peter."

"It's the least I can do for all you've done for May and me. If it weren't for you, I wouldn't have met the girl of my dreams."

I smiled. "I didn't do much. You had to woo her."

"Yeah, but you pointed me in the right direction."

"It was no problem."

Peter chuckled again. "I'll see you later, Eliza."

"Bye, Peter. Tell May I miss her."

"Will do."

I hung up and immediately called Jessica back.

"Mr. Smead's office. This is Jessica. How may I help you?"

"Jessica, this is Eliza."

"Ms. Trust! Good news I hope?"

"Yes. We will both be there this afternoon."

"Okay, thank you, Jessica."

"See you this afternoon."

I hung up and took a deep breath before picking up my mug. I should never do business before my first cup of coffee. Especially after drinking a whole bottle of wine the night before. I felt the ache in my head lessen as I drank from my mug. Coffee really was life-giving. What would the world do without it? Sleep forever, probably, I mused.

I made my way into the living room and over to the blinds, which were to the left of my television. I set my mug down to pull up the drawstrings, letting in the light of the morning sun. The view wasn't anything special. It over-looked the parking lot at the back of the building, but behind the lot was a small public park that was usually filled with children in the summer, but was now barren of their joyous screams and laughter.

Beyond that was the street, and it was filled with morning commuters, honking belligerently, trying to part traffic like Moses parted the Red Sea. I picked my Garfield mug back up and took a sip, humming softly to myself. It had been a long while since I'd had a calm morning. All this demons and angels mumbo jumbo wasn't good for my stress level.

How long had June dealt with all of it? She always seemed

to have an inner peace about her, a calmness, a stillness that couldn't be broken. Though I had broken it a few times, she still recovered quickly.

How did she do it? *Why* did she do it? I took another sip from my mug and leaned against the radiator. It hadn't kicked on in a few days. My heat was probably turned off. I would need to call my landlord, I thought absently. June didn't feel the cold or the heat. She was dead. Frozen in time. Dead, but not dead. She was still warm to the touch, and she could still feel things. That kiss...

I ran my fingers along my bottom lip. It still tingled at the memory of it. My bottom lip still hurt from where our teeth had met and cut it. That kiss had hurt in more ways than one. It made me feel things; confess things that I wasn't sure were true. Were they my feelings? Truly mine? Was it possible to fall in love with someone so quickly? Was it even that quickly?

She said she had waited three millennia to kiss me. Had she never kissed me in any of my past lives? God, it was so weird to think about having lived a different life but to have had the same soul. Is what I was feeling the result of a buildup of emotions over the course of several lifetimes? Or were they all authentically my feelings? Did I really love June West, my Grim Reaper? Would I ever know?

I took another sip of my coffee and looked up into the sky. It looked cold outside, but standing in my living room with my radiator turned off, I had never felt warmer.

CHAPTER NINE

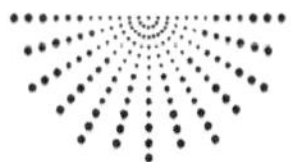

"*R*ight this way, Ms. Trust," a woman not much older than myself said as she directed me down a hallway.

"You're Jessica, right? Henry's assistant?"

She paused and nodded. "Please, call me Jess. I don't think we were ever formally introduced." She held out her hand.

"Then I insist that you call me Eliza. You can't be much older than me. It would be strange not to." I chuckled and reached out to clasp her offered hand. When we touched, a static shock seemed to transfer into my hand and up my arm, making it numb for a brief moment. I tried to pull back, but Jessica held me tightly. I looked up at her questioningly, only to see her eyes seemed to be glazed over, as if she wasn't quite all there at the moment. It was disconcerting. This all happened in the span of a few seconds before Jessica was back to normal, and squeezed my hand once before releasing me.

"Looks can be deceiving, Eliza. You should be careful who you offer your hand to."

I frowned, unsettled, as the same feeling of reality shifting around me disorientated me. I slowly nodded. "I'll keep that in mind."

Like a light switch, Jessica smiled brightly and the tension between us lifted instantly. "Good, now that we are introduced, how about I take you to Mr. Smead so you can sign that contract?"

I followed her through a side door leading away from the gallery and into a hallway with several office spaces. We paused in front of an open door. Entering, I was greeted by Henry, as well as two other men, one of which was Peter. They all stood as I entered.

"Sorry, am I late?"

Henry shook his head and led me over to the seat next to Peter. "Not at all, Ms. Trust. We were all just early. Your lawyer was just asking us some preliminary questions about the contract, but now that you are here, we can begin negotiations. Please, take a seat."

I smiled, trying to shake off the nerves. This would be my first major contract with a big gallery. I was good at dealing with negotiating industrial machinery, or deals that would better my current company at the time, but those all dealt with things I knew the value of. Angela was always telling me I was a talented artist; the problem was that I didn't entirely believe that, and now I was going to negotiate the value of something subjective—my art, my talent, and my value. I smiled at my lawyer.

"Hello, Peter."

He nodded. "Eliza, it's good to see you."

Henry took a seat. "Well, gentlemen and lady, shall we begin?"

Three hours. It took three hours to sign one contract. Despite Henry's upbeat personality, he was a true businessman. I could see why Philo's had made a name for itself and was known to house some of the most renowned artists in Seattle. If it wasn't for Peter, I don't know if I would have been able to navigate the contract, let alone walk away with what I thought was a great deal. Henry wasn't unreasonable, but he was aggressive behind his charming smiles. He still believed in treating his artists right, and the aggressiveness, I could deal with. It was when I had to decide how much I was worth to the gallery that I floundered and Peter had to take control.

We walked out of the office space and Henry shook my hand before shaking Peter's. "It was great doing business with you both. I look forward to speaking with you soon, Ms. Trust, about your future show. I have some great ideas to run by you."

"Me too, Henry." I smiled through exhaustion.

"Great! I'll have Jess call you with the details."

"Thanks," I said. I was mentally exhausted, and my couch, along with my TV dinner, was calling my name. That, or my bed. I couldn't tell which was calling louder. I needed to be home to decide which was more important. My caffeine kick had fizzled out after the first hour of negotiations.

"Eliza."

I turned to Peter.

"Can I walk you out?"

Smiling, I nodded, and he fell into step beside me.

"I think that all went well. Are you happy with the outcome?" Peter asked.

I sighed. "I'm happy with it. I guess I'm still in shock. I can't believe I'll have my show here. It's—"

"Amazing? A dream come true?" he finished.

I nodded. "Yeah."

Peter said, "I'm happy for you, Eliza. You know, May and I have been worried about you."

"Why?"

"May spoke to Angela about a week ago and said she mentioned you were having a hard time."

"Oh."

He raised his hands placatingly. "She didn't go into details. Just mentioned you were struggling a little bit with some things that had happened recently."

I nodded, and he opened the door leading back into the main gallery.

"Are you?" he asked.

"Struggling?"

Peter nodded. I thought for a moment. Things had been tough lately. The word *intense* came to mind.

Shrugging, I said, "Nothing I can't handle."

Peter touched my shoulder gently, making me pause mid-step and turn to meet his concerned gaze.

"You would tell if it wasn't, right? If you were in trouble?"

Peter had always been like a big brother to me—or at least he tried to be after I turned him down and pointed out May. Before that, I was more like his older sister, bailing him out of tough situations. May had been good for him and his development into a responsible person. His attempts to big brother me were nice sometimes, but there were just some things you couldn't tell your big brother, and my life was becoming one big secret after the other.

"Everything is all right, Peter. Thanks for asking but I'm a big girl, and I can handle whatever life throws at me."

He smiled. "Yeah, I guess you're right. You always were the responsible one. I just worry sometimes."

We made our way to the exit and Peter pushed the door open for me only so I could crash into someone. "Sorry!"

"We really need to stop running into each other like this," Gabriel smiled.

I felt the hot burn of anger as I met his gaze. His eyebrows rose.

"You!"

"Hello, Eliza. It's nice to see you again."

"I want to have a word with you," I sneered, as I thought of how June had been hurt because of the man in front of me. I knew June told me to forget about it, but seeing him here before me with his charming faux smile just rubbed me the wrong way. How dare he! After what he did.

Gabriel frowned, but Peter cut him off before he could respond. "Eliza, is this guy bothering you?"

"You could say that."

Gabriel's features momentarily darkened before he smirked. "I just wanted to offer to buy you a coffee again. But I guess you're busy."

I was going to regret this, but I couldn't let him get away with what he had done to June. "You know what? I'd like to get that coffee."

His eyebrows rose again. "Yeah?"

"You owe me one. I might as well cash in. Besides, I have something I want to speak to you about."

Gabriel held out his arm. "I'll drive."

I moved forward but was stopped by Peter's hand on my elbow. "Are you sure, Eliza?"

I hesitated before the image of June's back flashed through my mind and I squared my shoulders. "I'm sure."

He nodded and let go. "Be careful."

I smiled and walked past Gabriel, refusing to take his offered arm. He frowned but led me over to his red Ford Mustang parked in one of the patrons' reserved spaces. We drove in silence. Gabriel attempted to start several conversations, but I refused to speak with him until I was ready. Instead, I silently fumed in the passenger's seat until we reached Belltown. I was relieved when he pulled up to the familiar cafe at the marketplace where we'd first met. I didn't speak until I had a steaming cup of coffee in my hand and we were sitting outside on the patio.

"So, Eliza, what did you want to talk about?"

"What are you?"

He smiled. "I thought it would be apparent."

"It's not."

His smile fell. "I'm an angel."

I nodded. "But, you hurt June. Why? Aren't you supposed to be the good guy?"

His smile disappeared. "That woman overstepped her boundaries. I simply made sure she wouldn't do it again."

"By tearing her apart?" My voice rose.

"She was dealt with appropriately."

"Oh, yeah?" I said, and stood as my voice rose once again.

"I only did what was within my rights. She broke the rules, and I made sure she was punished. I didn't do anything wrong, Eliza. Surely, you must see that. The soul stealer was in the wrong."

"I see everything perfectly," I sneered, taking the lid off my still steaming coffee and dumping it on his lap.

"Hey!" He jumped up.

"You're an asshole. I'm just exercising my right to put you in *your* place. Surely, you must see that?"

Gabriel wiped furiously at his pants with a napkin.

"Thanks for the coffee. I feel much better; refreshed, even."

He looked up and there was a wildness in his eyes. "I'll make you pay for this."

My heart skipped and I took a step back. His features darkened and Gabriel looked every bit the avenging angel he must have been as he spoke. "This is the part where you run." He lunged.

I screamed and jumped back, knocking a chair over.

Dodging tables and customers, I took off down the sidewalk. Shit! Did I really just do that? I laughed even as I ran for my life. Who knew dumping coffee on an asshole was so liberating?

I could hear his heavy footfalls behind me and I pushed my legs harder. People jumped out of my way as I charged down the sidewalk and through the marketplace. It was late afternoon, so the lunch crowd was about, filling the streets. I pushed and shoved people even as I sensed Gabriel gaining on me. What I needed was a way to either put some distance between us or a place to hide. Glancing around the busy streets, I spotted an alleyway hidden between an apple booth and a pineapple vendor. There! I lunged, pushing a senior man out of the way in the process. He cursed at me even as I dove into the opening, escaping the crowd. Leaning heavily against the brick walls I tried to catch my breath, only to look up and realize there was no outlet.

"Shit!"

A deep, mocking laughter made me spin around, coming face-to-face with a very pissed off angel.

"I'VE TRIED TO BE A NICE GUY, BUT YOU'VE TESTED MY patience, Eliza."

I snorted even as my legs wobbled. "Your head is so far up your ass you can't even see your own shit."

He frowned. "That's not very ladylike. You're so vulgar."

He advanced. I stepped back, bumping up against the solid stone of the wall. A dead end.

He smirked. "Too bad your harlot isn't here to save you."

"Shut up!"

He grinned. "Did I offend you? Good, you deserve it after

the way you've treated me. I'm next in line to be an archangel, you know."

"Did they make a mistake?"

He frowned. "Cute. You're my last assignment. All I have to do is take your soul and claim it for my side, stealing away its essence, then I'll dump what's left of you back on that soul stealer. If I do that, I'll be promoted, and I'll finally gain the recognition that I deserve as the powerful angel I was born to be."

"More like inflated, egotistical bastard."

He frown deepened. I guess he didn't get my sense of humor. "I didn't expect you to recognize greatness even if it hit you in the face. Your soul is already tainted. Truthfully, I pity you."

"I'd rather have a tainted soul than choose your side!"

"So, you're already planning on choosing the demons' side? Well, I guess this worked out in my favor then. I've made sure that we won't be interrupted for a while. It will be plenty of time to kill you and enjoy doing it."

"What did you do to June?"

He smirked, "Not enough. I just made a couple of suggestions to people looking to move up in the company. Nothing Death won't eventually figure out how to handle."

He stepped closer, and I finally felt the panic I had been fending off overwhelm me at the realization that I was alone; June wasn't going to save me this time.

"How would you like to die? I prefer the slow kill, but I'm benevolent."

I opened my mouth to tell him to go to Hell when his shadow suddenly moved and grew, morphing into a new shape as it rose from the concrete to stand between us. It grew until it stood a head above Gabriel, then it solidified. Kaleb stood between me and my would-be murderer. The enemy of my enemy was my friend, I mused. *I'll take what I can get.*

Kaleb smirked. He had a toothpick in one hand and seemed to be cleaning out his teeth as if he had just enjoyed a meal. What do demons even eat? I shuddered at the thought.

"Gabe, long time no see. How have you been?" His smooth voice cut through the tension placatingly.

"It's no business of yours, bottom feeder!" the angel spat.

Kaleb seemed unconcerned. "Ah, self-righteous as always, I see. Good to know some things never change."

"Get out of my way, demon!"

Kaleb shrugged. "You're welcome to try and move me. I'll warn you, though, I'm still ever so famished. Drug addicts are always a bit on the skinny side. They never fill one such as myself completely, if you know what I mean."

"Why would I?"

The demon looked surprised, as if just seeing Gabriel for the first time. "Oh, pardon my rudeness. I mistook you for one of my underlings. Your soul is as black as the soot on my boot."

Kaleb laughed as Gabriel growled and charged at him, tackling the demon to the ground. I screamed and jumped back, pushing myself as close to the wall as I could. It was as fascinating as it was terrifying to watch the two men roll around in the dirt. They kept flickering in and out, transforming from gruesome angelic creatures back into their human disguises.

One minute Gabriel was pounding Kaleb's face in, and the next the demon was breaking the angel's arm, only for it to mend back together immediately. After a very pointy tooth whizzed by my head, I realized it might be a good idea to escape while I still could. I didn't know what Kaleb hoped to gain from saving me and I didn't want to stick around to find out, either. Slowly, I moved along the edge of the alley until I made it past the dueling supernatural beings, then took off as fast as I could. They didn't even notice me leave.

As I rounded the corner three blocks away from the fighting and finally out of the marketplace, I pulled out my cell phone. I scrolled down to the number saved by the name Grim Reaper and clicked the speed dial. It rang. And rang. And rang.

"Come on, June, pick up."

By the sixth ring, I was in full-blown panic mode. Then, it clicked.

"Hello?" June sounded breathless.

"June! Oh, thank God. Are you okay? Are you all right, June?"

"Eliza? What's wrong?" Her voice was a little more steady.

"Gabriel was trying to kill me, and he said you were in trouble. I thought you were getting beaten again. I was so scared. You're not hurt, are you? I don't know what I would do if you were hurt because of me again. Oh, Jesus! You're hurt aren't you—"

"Eliza! Calm down. You have to calm down, honey. I don't understand what you're saying. Take a deep breath."

"Oh my God. I can't breathe. June, I can't breathe. I'm running, and I can't breathe, and you could be dead!"

I tripped but caught myself on the concrete wall of a building. I leaned my whole body weight on it as my vision swam. Several people gave me a wide berth on the sidewalk.

"Eliza, I need you to breathe."

"I can't!" I wheezed.

"Listen to me. Listen to the sound of my voice, Eliza. Focus on my breathing and my voice. Can you do that, honey?"

"I'll try."

"Good. I'm okay. Nothing happened that I can't handle. I'm not hurt, and I'm fine. Gabriel didn't do anything to me directly. I had suspected that he was behind the sudden coup but it didn't hurt me. Death just has everyone on lockdown right now, but I'm going to see you as soon as I can. I need you to tell me what is happening calmly or I can't help you. Can you do that for me? Can you tell me what happened?"

I nodded, and my breathing began to even out at the soothing tones she was using. "Yeah. I'm okay now."

"Good. Tell me what happened."

"Gabriel, he tried to kill me, but Kaleb stepped in and stopped him. I just barely managed to escape while they were fighting one another."

I heard her curse. "Are you okay? Did either of them hurt you?"

"No, I'm fine."

I heard her sigh.

"But I'm scared, June. I don't know what to do."

There was a pause on her side of the line followed by some muffled voices yelling. Then I heard June curse again. "Eliza?"

"Yeah?"

"You're going to have to do what I say, okay?"

"What do you want me to do? What's wrong?"

"Nothing I can't handle, but you're in danger. You can't go back to your apartment. Both Kaleb and Gabriel know where you live, and you'll be alone. You're going to have to walk around the city and stay in crowded places, but that will only hold them off for a while. If what you say is true and they've broken the rules, then anything is fair game, and I wouldn't put it past them to send their minions after you."

I shuddered. "What should I do, June?"

She was silent for a moment, as if she was thinking, then she sighed. "Eliza, I can't come to you right now. I can't leave where I am. I'm going to need you to come to me."

"Okay, I can do that. Where are you?"

"Honey, I'm in the Otherworld."

"The Otherworld? Is that a club?"

"Not quite."

"Well, how do I get there?"

"Eliza, you're going to have to go through a portal to get here."

"A portal? Right, of course. Why not? It's the Otherworld, after all…" I could hear the hysteria building up in my voice.

"Eliza, take a deep breath." I did as she instructed.

"Are you still with me?"

I nodded. "Yeah, sorry. It's been a long fucking day."

"I know, but I need you to hold it together. Can you do that for me?"

"Yeah. I make no promises, but I'll do my best."

"That's all I ask."

"What do I need to do? Where do I find this portal?"

"Listen carefully, and do exactly what I tell you to, and it will work out…somehow."

"That sounds reassuring."

"It's the best I can offer. This hasn't been done in a long time."

"I'm not going to die from this, am I?"

"No, but…"

"But?"

"You might be ripped apart. But it's not that big of a deal. The percentage of that happening is low."

"I don't feel so good, June."

"Just do what I say, and it will be fine."

"Are you sure? You don't sound sure."

"Trust me, Eliza."

I paused and looked around at the people walking past me without giving me a second glance. I was no one to them; just another face in the crowd. But to the woman on the other end of the line, I was someone. An important someone that she has been protecting for a very long time. If there was one person I could put my trust in, it should be the woman that has spent every one of my past lives watching out for me. I smiled. "I do trust you. I trust you with all my heart, June."

I could hear the smile in her voice. "Good. Thank you. Now, here's what you need to do."

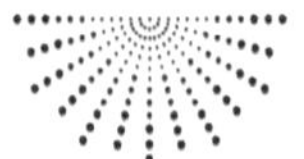

CHAPTER TEN

Of course, it was in the old city. The old city was known as a portal hotspot, after all. It was no big deal. Honey, where are you going today? To the old city. I hear there's a new portal down there! Okay, have fun, but be back in time for dinner! Shit, I'm losing my mind.

June explained that I would have to go down into the old city, also known as the Seattle Underground. It was what remained of the old Seattle after the Great Fire of 1889. Seattle was essentially rebuilt on top of itself afterward, and all that was left was the ruin of history. I had taken a tour of the Underground when I first moved to the city as a freshman at Washington University. It had been scary and creepy, but it also helped my love for Seattle grow as I learned how the city I knew today came to be. It wasn't that surprising that something supernatural would exist in such a historic place.

The first problem I faced was getting there. Gabriel had brought me back to Belltown to get coffee, and the closest entrance to the Underground was about sixteen minutes by bus from where I currently was. Thus, leading me to the only real challenge I had. I couldn't avoid public transportation anymore. I finally had to take the bus. It was a crowded enough place that I wasn't in any danger of Kaleb or Gabriel attacking me, and it was the quickest way of getting to my destination.

Double shit!

Standing, I waited impatiently. Glancing down at my watch told me it was coming any minute. I sighed. "Okay, I can do this. It's easy. I just put one foot in front of the other, then I'll sit down toward the front like I always do. Easy. The worst thing that can happen is someone farts next to me."

The hum of the bus brought me out of my pep talk.

I whispered, "Okay, girl. You got this."

The bus stopped, the doors opened, and I froze. My mind just went blank and the sounds around me disappeared as I stared at the black grooves of the first step. Someone shoved me from behind. Suddenly, the hum was loud, my heart was pounding in my chest, and I was shaking. *I can't do this. Shit! I can't do this.*

"Miss? Are you getting on?"

I looked up and met the kind gaze of the bus driver.

"What?" I gasped.

He smiled. "Are you going to climb on?"

I swallowed, getting my breathing under control, and shook my head. "I don't know if I can."

He chuckled. "Sure you can. Just place one foot on the first step and move on from there."

"I..." I trailed. My palms were sweaty.

He stood, and walking to the top of the stairs, held out his hand. "Here, let me help you. Sometimes, the first step is the hardest. We all just need a bit of help to get us going."

I swallowed again. Nodding, I reached out and gripped the offered hand. It was big, rough, and strong as he pulled me forward. One step. Two steps. Three steps.

"There you go." He led me over to a seat toward the front and helped me sit down.

I gripped his hand tight; I was still trembling. He patted my hand, squeezed it reassuringly, then let go. "We should be on our way now. Places to go, things to do, people to see."

He turned back to the few other passengers in the back. This stop was after the hub, so I wasn't surprised at there only being a few people on board.

He nodded. "Sorry about that, folks."

Taking his seat behind the wheel, he shifted out of park and the bus began to move again. Glancing out the window, I flexed my hand in my lap and took a deep breath. The city whipped by, the bus hummed, and my stop was only two stops away. The most important thing, though, was that I was okay. I was on a bus, after six weeks of avoiding them, and I was all right. I was just fine.

***

THE BUS DROPPED ME OFF ABOUT A BLOCK AWAY FROM PIONEER Square. I had to push through the afternoon crowd to finally reach my destination. I pushed through the doors of Bill Speidel's Underground Tours and walked into a lobby filled with eager tourists.

"Single file, everyone, please! Follow me in single file!" a young woman called out from the front of the line.

I jogged over to the front counter where a teenage boy was blowing bubbles with his gum and playing on his cell phone. I slapped a twenty down on the counter, startling him off of his phone.

"I want to go on that tour!" I pointed to the group following the woman down a flight of stairs.

"Um…"

"Give me a ticket, now!"

He started from the intensity of my demand and the desperation in my voice and quickly jumped into action by taking my money and printing off a ticket. It only took him about five seconds before he was handing me what I requested,

"Enjoy, miss!" he called out as I jogged to catch up to the tour group that was still filing down the stairs.

"Sure!" I called out over my shoulder and hopped down the stairs, bringing up the rear of the tour group. At the end of the stairs were a set of double doors. As I pushed through them, a draft of cold air brushed against my face and through my hair. I walked into a dark hallway made of stone. It was almost like walking into a cave, as it was lit entirely by lamps and old, antique chandeliers.

"Please stay together! On your left, you'll see the remains of an old teller's box. Did you know…"

The woman continued to tell a humorous story of an adulterous teller as she led us down a wooden walkway. Several tourists were snapping photos with their smartphones and posting the pictures to some social media. I mused as I remembered being just like them on my first tour through the Underground.

I could still remember the history that my tour guide had imparted on me. After the Great Fire of 1889, a stage of the rebuilding of Pioneer Square took place. By that time, several laws had been passed on road and housing regulations. Thus what used to be the ground floor of a building suddenly became the basement, and so on.

Virtually an entire network of interconnected underground passageways that were once roads, as well as businesses, became a town beneath the city. Thus the Underground became a historic site. It wasn't until many years later that a very curious and brave man and his wife jumped through many hoops to begin giving tours of it to prove the historical value of it that the Underground became popular. Now, thousands of tours are given annually, and the place was preserved.

The tour guide led us across a walkway and pointed to the right. "To your right, you will see what used to be an old parlor. It was commonly frequented by travelers passing through Pioneer Square. Did you know..." She jumped into another wild story of life on Pioneer Square before the fire.

I tuned her out as I glanced around. This was where June told me to separate from the group. The other tourists were too busy on their phones to notice when I ducked through the small opening between the guardrails and walked across unsteady, cracked concrete. I quickly made my way to the parlor as the tour guide led the group down another walkway.

I pushed through the dimly lit remains and walked through cobwebs. "Gross!" I muttered as I walked through the overturned tables and made my way to what remained of the bar. It was nothing more than rusted metal and wood now. I pushed past it until I reached a hidden door in the back. Gently, I edged it open. It creaked ominously and a gust of cold air burst out, causing me to cough from the dust that came along with it.

"The things I do..." I trailed off and walked over to a stone wall. There was nothing special about the wall besides the white chalked circle on the center of it. Hesitantly, I rested my hands on the circle.

"Here goes nothing!" I set my shoulders, taking a deep breath before I spoke the words June had made me memorize.

"Door to ice, door to fire, the dead demands entry to the next plane, grant me entry, it is my desire!"

As I spoke the last words, I felt an insistent pull on my hands before the room around me blurred, and I was being pulled through time and space. The feeling of leaving my stomach behind, as well as a wrongness, filled me, and I closed my eyes. It felt like someone was trying to pull my soul from my body! I wrapped my arms around my torso to hold myself together, but before I could gain control over my limbs again, soft, warm arms were suddenly wrapped around me and the smell of burnt cinnamon filled the air. I was pulled into a soft body.

A quiet voice sighed next to my ear, "Eliza."

I wrapped my arms around the solid figure. "June!"

She pulled back and studied me "Are you all right?"

"I think so—" Suddenly, my stomach caught up and flipped, and I pushed away from her before I emptied my breakfast on the tiled floor.

"You'll get used to it. First-timers always struggle with their first jump," she soothed, and held my hair out of the way.

I gained control of myself after a few minutes and leaned against her heavily. "Where am I?" I asked, and took in my surroundings only to shudder as I realized that June was once again wearing her bone mask. The room we were in seemed to be a bathroom, if the stalls and sinks were any indication. "And what did I go through?"

She pointed behind me to a mirror. "That's a portal that physical beings can pass through without the aid of a bone walker. Don't ask why it's in a bathroom, just be thankful it's in the women's and not the men's."

"But I thought you didn't need to eat?"

She smiled. "I don't. The bathrooms are sort of a joke. They're mostly used as a place to escape from the office."

"The office?"

She shrugged. "You'll see what I mean. But for now, I need you to put these on."

June produced a Halloween mask along with a hoodie, practically from thin air.

"What are those for?"

She pointed to her face. "No one can know that you're human. It won't end well. Put these on quickly. We have to get you out of this building before Death figures out that I brought you here."

"Death? Like the dead Death? The real Grim Reaper?"

"Yes, now hurry!" She shoved the mask and hoodie into my hands. I nodded dumbly and slid the plastic mask over my face before shrugging on the black hooded sweatshirt. I belatedly realized that I had been cold.

"Where am I, June?"

She grabbed my hand and pulled me behind her. "This is the Otherworld."

"The Otherworld?"

June nodded. "The realm in which spirits rule. It's Death's realm."

"Am I dead?"

"No. You're still alive. Come on." She pulled me through the bathroom doors and out into the hallway.

I looked around, only to see an open space of cubicles and hear the sound of phones ringing. The only thing it was missing was the smell of coffee.

"The office," I mused.

A man walked past us, and I gasped when I saw the lower half of his face was covered in a mask of white bone. He nodded to us politely as he walked by holding a stack of papers in his hands.

"Morning!" he chirped, and the bone along his jaw clacked together, making me shudder. I saw June nod curtly to him before dragging me faster.

"Are we in an office building?"

"Actually, it's Death's main headquarters," June whispered as she pulled me along.

We walked down a hallway covered in windows. I glanced out of them, only to stumble forward. The world outside was nothing like where I came from. The sky was a peach pink, and there was no sun. There seemed to be a courtyard down below us. The strangest thing, though, was that instead of there being a skyline of several neighboring buildings, there was nothing but vast, open fields; what looked like blue grass for miles upon miles on end.

"Come on, Eliza. We have to hurry." I hadn't realized I had stopped until June was pulling me forward again.

"Outside—"

She nodded. "I know. It's different."

"Yeah. Different," I whispered as June dragged us toward an elevator.

She pushed the call button and we waited for a moment before the doors slid open, only to reveal several businessmen and women all wearing different types of bone masks. Some had the top of their faces covered while others had their bottom halves covered, but none had a full-faced mask like June's. They were all shapes and sizes. While June's mask looked like a human skull, the people on the elevator had masks representing animals. One man had a long beak covering the bottom half of his jaw while a woman had what looked like hamster teeth jutting past her mouth. One man even had a crescent moon tattooed on the center of his mask's forehead.

I quietly gasped as June pulled me forward into the elevator. The doors were beginning to close but a hand suddenly shot in, making them open again. June stiffened next to me as a man with a mask covering only the top half of his face climbed on and stood next to her. I studied him closer from the corner of my eye. The bone covering the top of his face was white and looked much like a human's, but there was an insignia of some type printed on each side of his head when he glanced down at me. It seemed to be of a small, blue circle with a white circle within it, and a small black circle at the very center, almost like the pupil of an eye.

An awkward tension filled the elevator as several people fidgeted and twitched. My hand tightened around June's. At the next floor the doors opened and everyone besides June, the man, and I, hurried off. June stepped forward, but the man's hand shot out and pulled her back.

"Now, June. Where do you think you're going?"

Her eyes were hard when they turned to meet his. "Matt."

His green eyes seemed to have a hidden humor. "Death is most eager to meet our guest. You wouldn't want to keep him waiting, would you?"

She shrugged his hand off but stepped back into the elevator. "I find the thought of him being anything other than bored, disturbing."

Matt chortled, "As do we all."

He reached forward and pushed the button for B13 before studying me. "Hello, Eliza. You won't need that Halloween mask now; it was a nice touch though. I wouldn't have suspected anything if Death hadn't warned me beforehand."

I glanced at June, but she seemed to have found something interesting on the wall to study. I turned back to the man while taking off the mask. I set it down on the floor before turning back to the man. "You know me?"

He nodded. "Usually when I see you, you're nothing but a spirit, so I'm not surprised you don't remember me. It's nice to meet you officially when you're a whole person. I'm sorry it couldn't be under better circumstances."

"Who are you?"

"You can call me Matt. I'm Death's assistant."

I frowned. "You don't hear that job title every day."

He chuckled. "No, I'm sure you don't."

The elevator dinged and the doors opened. He motioned forward. "Right this way please."

June pulled me forward as we followed Matt down the dimly lit hallway. It seemed to drop in temperature as we progressed. We paused in front of an ominous wooden door with what looked like gargoyles engraved into it, before I heard a muffled voice call out and Matt pushed the doors open. June dropped my hand as we entered.

The room was tastefully decorated with a Victorian décor, and sitting at the far end of the room, behind a monstrous cherry wood desk, was a thin, sickly, pale man with a bored expression on his face.

Matt bowed. "Death, I have brought them as requested. Will you need anything else?"

Death absently waved his hand and Matt bowed again before leaving the office.

Death sighed. "So you've brought the Lamb of Essence into my realm?"

I glanced at June, but she seemed to have turned to stone beside me. I turned back to the pale man. "What's going on?"

"She didn't tell you?" Death asked.

I glanced at June out of the corner of my eye. She was studying the carpet. I looked back to Death. "Will you?"

He picked a piece of imaginary lint off of his impeccable suit jacket. "I suppose so. It's not too complicated. Do you know what it means to be the Lamb?"

I shook my head. "Not quite."

"Very well. June and you were souls that one day became extraordinarily bright."

"What do you mean?"

"One could say you were luminous and filled with positive energy the likes of which we have never seen before."

I frowned. "Do you know why?"

He shrugged. "I suspect it was the result of the love you share for one another, even before June signed my contract."

I blushed.

"So, as I was saying, your souls were vibrant, and I needed a powerful soul to give the all-important duty of the Lamb of Essence. You see, Eliza, the Lamb must keep the balance of the physical world and the Otherworld. It needs a lot of positive energy to accomplish that and when June signed my contract, becoming an eternal soul, the energy from the both of you increased exponentially. If I remember correctly, you lit up the whole of the Otherworld like a supernova." He said this all in his apathetic tone, so I wasn't able to determine how he felt about it. He didn't seem to hold any grudges against June or me. Then, why did he do this to us? Maybe this all happened as a result of my ever-present bad luck.

"What contract did June sign?"

His dark eyes met my gaze and a chill ran down my spine. "She signed the bone walker contract, but it had a little extra to it."

"What extra?"

"Since you are both soul mates, you each hold equal dominion over each other's souls. Soul mates are two halves of a whole, after all. When June signed herself over to me, she also signed your soul into my service as collateral. Therefore, you have indirectly signed yourself over to me. As the Lamb of Essence, your life essence is used to tip the scale of energy one way or the other. It was the only way at the time that I could stop the fighting between the angels and the demons, which would have eventually destroyed both the physical world as well as the Otherworld." He sighed as if speaking was some great chore, and it probably was. He was most likely used to using as few words as possible to order people around.

"But why would she do that?"

He shrugged. "You'll have to ask her."

I turned to June, who had yet to look up from her inspection of the floor. "June?"

She met my gaze. Her gray eyes blazed in barely restrained rage. I stepped back and she softened slightly before turning back to Death.

"Are we here for a reason? Or, are we free to leave?"

Death nodded. "Yes, of course you are here for a reason. You know bringing a being from the physical world here is against the rules. Punishable by fifty lashes, if I remember correctly," he said thoughtfully.

"No!"

He looked to me. "No?"

I moved to block June from his view. "I won't let you hurt her again."

He seemed confused by my words. "But she broke the rules. There must be a punishment, or others will start doing it, and that would be a disaster."

I shook my head. "It's my fault."

"Eliza!" June grabbed my shoulder, but I shook her off.

"Punish me!"

Death sighed. "That simply won't do. As the Lamb of Essence, you're impervious to the punishments we inflict here in the Otherworld. I cannot punish you. It's against the rules."

I squared my shoulders. I might regret this later. "Then make a contract with me."

Death frowned. "A contract?"

I nodded. "I want to make one with you."

June grabbed my arm. "No, Eliza! What are you saying?"

I tried to break free from her grasp, but her grip was iron. I turned back to Death. "There must be something you want?"

"What exactly is it that you want?" he asked in his bored tone.

I glanced back at June. She was pleading with her eyes, but I had to do this. For my sake; for her sake. I turned back to Death. "I want you to free us."

"Free you?"

"Yes."

He paused, and I watched as some strange emotion entered his eyes. It was something sinister. Something cold and slimy.

"A contract to free yourself from your job as the Lamb of Essence," he stated.

I nodded. "That's right."

He held out his hand.

"And you can't hurt June ever again."

Death nodded. "Let us shake on it then."

I stepped forward but was held back. I met stormy, gray eyes. "Let go."

Her gaze hardened but her voice was steady. "No."

"June, let go."

"You don't know what you're doing. I'd rather be beaten for all of eternity than let you shake his hand."

I could feel the familiar sting in the corners of my eyes. "Please, June. Let me do this for you."

She shook her head. "Never."

Tears began to fall down my cheeks. "Let go."

She didn't reply, but her grip tightened almost painfully.

"This won't do. Interference is not allowed." Death

clapped his hands twice, and suddenly June was on the other side of the room being held by two burly men with bone masks. Henchmen, I assumed.

"Eliza, shall we?" His apathetic tone had something hidden in it that made me hesitate a moment. With one last look at June, I stepped forward.

"Don't do it, Eliza! Don't you dare shake his hand!" Her usually quiet voice was harsh and threatening. I could hear her struggling to break free even as I reached out and shook the pale and cold hand of Death. Something bit me as our hands met and I jerked mine back, tucking it into my chest.

"Ow! What was that?"

"What?" He tilted his head.

"You bit me!" I held my hand out as proof.

He didn't even look down. "No, I didn't."

"It's right—" I looked down, only to see unbroken skin. The only proof I had that I didn't imagine the incident was the throbbing pain left behind.

"But—"

Death cut me off by clapping again, and I turned to see June alone, once again studying the carpet.

"Now that you have signed with blood, the contract will not fade; you are under Death's dominion until Death is remade."

I met the bored gaze of Death and watched in terror as he smiled wickedly for a moment before it was gone and all that remained was apathy.

"What was that?"

He shrugged. "I'm required by the contract to say it. But, onto more important things. You have a job to do."

"A job?"

"I have some things I want to be acquired, and you must both get them for me or I can't uphold my end of the contract."

"But I didn't sign anything."

He absently waved his hand. "Do you want your contract upheld or not?"

"What exactly do I get out of it?"

"Didn't you clearly state your terms?"

"But I didn't get to see them in writing."

He nodded. "One doesn't always get what one wants."

"But—" I was cut off by June gently touching my shoulder. She didn't look at me but instead met Death's gaze. "What do you need?"

He sighed. "A tear from an archangel and the blood of the Morning Star."

June nodded. "Is that all?"

"That is all that I require."

"Are we now free to leave?"

He shrugged. "I suppose."

June grabbed my hand and dragged me out of Death's office. She continued to drag me all the way to the elevator in silence. When the doors opened, she glared at the people still in it. "Get out!"

They scurried like ants. Then she all but threw me into it. I stumbled inside, catching my balance on the bar. "Hey! What was that for?"

She turned her back to me and pushed the button for the lobby.

"I'm talking to you!" I reached for her shoulder, only for her to spin around and push me up against the back of the elevator. Her eyes were like a raging storm as they bore into mine.

"June?" I whispered.

She glared, pushing her body further into mine. Then she was kissing me. Her mouth was claiming mine and forcing her tongue into my warm depths. June held my hands prisoner with one of hers against the wall. I groaned as the other trailed under my shirt and lightly scratched her fingernail along my stomach. She nipped at my lip while pushing her hips into mine.

I was lost in her relentless onslaught of my mouth, but every time I tried to touch her, to pull her closer or push her away, I wasn't sure, she would push my hands away. A carnal sound escaped my lips when a firm thigh settled between my legs.

"June!" I moaned, and couldn't stop myself from grinding helplessly against her.

Then, she was gone. It was like having ice water dumped on me. She was missing, and I was a panting mess. I struggled to keep my balance and looked up at her only to be met with her back once again.

"What—" The doors opened and she walked off, leaving me and my racing heart to chase after her.

"June! Wait!" I jogged to catch up with her. I only managed to do so once we were outside the building and I grabbed her hand. She slowed her gait to a stop. "June what was—"

I spun her around again only to see that the woman I had come to associate with unshakable strength was crying. Big, fat tears were flowing down her face. I was at a loss for words. She continued to cry silent tears as we stood outside in the courtyard that surrounded the building.

"June," I whispered, and reached out to cup her face.

"I…" She trailed off and furiously tried to wipe away her tears.

I pulled her into me. "It will be all right."

She pushed me away and her gaze was suddenly hard; stone-cold. "We have work to do." Then she walked away from me with tears still streaming down her face.

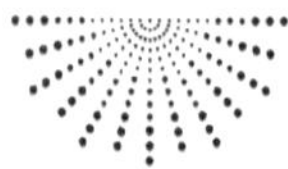

CHAPTER ELEVEN

I shook off my shock and chased after her again. Just as I grabbed her arm, the world around me shifted. Blurs of colors and shapes rushed by one second, only to stop the next. Suddenly, the loud, obnoxious sounds of rush hour Seattle filled my ears. It was disorientating after the stillness the Otherworld offered. I dropped June's arm and grabbed my stomach as it caught up a second too late. The next minute I was bent over and dry heaving. People quickly jumped out of my way.

My eyes watered as my stomach attempted to empty what wasn't there. It took me a moment to realize that there was a warm hand rubbing up and down my back and someone was holding my hair up. I looked up only to realize that June had somehow moved us into an alleyway.

"Are you okay?" she asked.

I nodded. "I think so."

"Good."

Then she was cold and walked away from me again.

"June! Stop it!" I grabbed her hand for the last time.

"Goddamnit, June! If you walk away from me one more

time I'm going to punch you." I held her hand, but she still wouldn't look at me.

"June, look at me. Quit being a little kid. We are grown up, and adults talk about things that are bothering them. So, talk to me."

Finally, she met my gaze, but I was stunned by the depth of pain revealed in hers. "Then why didn't you talk to me before you shook his hand?"

I frowned. "Death's hand?"

She nodded. "You said adults talk about things. You ignored me."

"I had to."

"No, you didn't."

"He was going to hurt you again." My grip on her hand tightened.

"It would have been better than what you did."

"How can you say that?"

"Eliza, I've been hurt before, and I'll be hurt again. It's part of the job. But what you did? You signed a contract with Death. Do you even realize what that means? There's no going back. You have to uphold your end of the deal or else..."

"Or else what?"

She shook her head. "It doesn't matter. We are going to do what he wants."

I released her hand. "I hate it when you do that."

She frowned. "What?"

I met her gaze, and I could feel my face getting hot. "You never tell me anything! You're always keeping things to yourself! I'm not a little kid, June. I can handle the truth, but you're always feeding me half-truths and trying to keep me safe by not telling me everything."

"That's unfair."

"Oh, yeah? Then tell me why you signed the bone walker

contract. Tell me what is happening to us. Why is all this happening now? Tell me everything I *should* know, not what you think I should know!"

June studied my face, and I could already feel the imaginary steam blowing out my ears as my temper ebbed away, leaving exhaustion in its wake. "I just don't want to be lied to anymore. Please."

She nodded. "Answer me one question."

"What?"

"Do you love me?"

I hesitated a moment. "I don't know."

Her face went blank, and she stilled. "What?"

I took a deep breath. "I said that I'm not sure if what I feel for you is real or not."

"But you said—"

"I know what I said, but I said it during a moment. Look, June; I've never liked anyone. I thought that I was asexual or something. It was both a source of relief and confusion when I met you and felt something. I don't mind that you're a woman. I'm cool with that. You being a bone walker threw me off, but I can accept that, too. But these things I feel for you? They are so intense—too intense. I've never wanted to be with someone the way I want to be with you, and it scares the shit out of me. I don't know you, but I've also known you for a really long time," I finished in a whisper.

June remained silent, her face still blank. Then she spoke. "Do you want to?"

I frowned. "Want to what?"

She gave me a small smile. "Do you want to know me?"

I paused, but I already had my answer. "God yes. I want to know everything about you. I want the chance to see if I can feel these things as I am now, not as I was. You love my soul, June. But can you honestly say that you love me, Eliza Trust?"

"Yes." She didn't even hesitate.

I smiled. "How can you be so sure?"

"Because I know you. You may change a little in every life as your soul matures, but the essence of you, what makes you who you are regardless of your upbringing or the time period you are born into; that is what I love. The way you look and your name may change, but you, Eliza, I love you, and nothing will ever change how I feel. You are my other half. I don't want to love another. All I've ever wanted was you."

My breath hitched as I watched the emotions play out on June's face, only to settle with the one that has always been present beneath the pain and sadness. Love was ever present whenever she gazed at me, and it never diminished.

"Then give me the chance to see you, June. Show me everything that you are without fear of whether I will accept you the way you accept me. Let me learn you like the back of my hand so I can answer your question of whether or not I love you. But all I can give you right now is that I care for you deeply and I want to know you. Is that enough for now? Please, can that be enough?"

She reached out and pulled my hand up to her mouth, where she kissed each knuckle before placing it above her heart. "It's more than enough. I'd wait an eternity for you if you asked it of me."

We stepped forward, and our lips met in a simple kiss. It was both light and filled with unspoken promises. I pulled back and smiled. "Thank you, June. Thank you for loving me."

She pressed her lips to my forehead and tightened her hold on my hand. "You couldn't stop me even if you tried."

I nodded. "I know."

"So will you tell me why you signed his contract?"

June stepped back and nodded. She took a deep breath. "I died. It was a very long time ago, but when I died, Death was there."

"You went to the Otherworld?"

She nodded. "I was a warrior in my past life. You don't know this, but not just anyone is offered the bone walker contract. You have to die a valiant death even to be considered for it. Only certain people can handle a position of such great power and not go insane from it. The bone walker contract is eternal, and the only way to escape it is for Death to nullify it. Or at least that's the only way I know of."

"So what happened?"

"When I died, I woke up in his office. It was as you saw it today and it was very disorientating, to say the least. I had never seen anything like it. He held out his hand to help me stand and warily, I took it. Then he bit me and the contract was signed."

"That's it?"

June nodded. "Death is known for his tricks. He will do anything to get what he wants, and as he stated earlier, he wanted our souls, and took the easiest route to obtain them."

"That slimy son of a bitch!"

She smiled. "You could say that. Do you see why I didn't want you to sign another contract? You may think you stated your terms clearly, but who knows what he has up his sleeve. No one ever knows what Death is planning, and I trust him about as far as I can throw him."

I frowned. "Do you think he has something planned?"

She shook her head. "I don't know, but it doesn't matter. You signed it, and now we have to keep your end of it, or else you will be subjected to a pain unimaginable."

"What do you mean?"

"No one knows what happens if you can't keep up your

end of a contract, but it's said that it's something so terrible that it blackens your soul. As a bone walker, we can see the color of a person's soul. The color tells us whether it should be reincarnated or not. A pure-white soul is given to the angels. Gray souls are within our jurisdiction and are reincarnated. But blackened souls, those are given to demons. They are souls that have made their choice to deny an angel's guidance and the chance at another life."

I nodded. "Okay. So how do we go about getting this archangel's tear and the blood?"

June smiled. "Well, time in the Otherworld is different than the physical world. It moves neither forward nor backward, but it doesn't stand still."

"What does that even mean?"

She laughed. "No one really knows, but I do know that Gabriel has been promoted to the position of archangel while we were in the Otherworld."

I frowned. "I thought he had to catch me first?"

She shrugged. "One of the bone walkers I get my information from mentioned that Gabriel's father convinced the other angels that his son was worthy of the position and they accepted his reasoning. So Gabriel was promoted."

"But what about the blood of the Morning Star? How do we get that?"

"Kaleb."

"Kaleb? Is he actually the devil?"

June shook her head. "No, but he was a soul made physical by the bone and blood of Lucifer. His blood is the closest we can get to the real thing. We just have to hope it's enough."

I nodded. "But do you know where we can find either of them?"

"Since they were the representatives for the competition this time, I was given a sort of tracking device for both of them. It only tells me the general direction they are in, but I've been following them and know most of the places they like to hunt. The problem will be if they have gone back to their realms. I can't enter the demons' or the angels' realm without permission."

"Are they here?"

June closed her eyes and nodded after a moment. "Kaleb is hunting, while Gabriel is in the direction of the gallery."

I frowned. "What do you mean by hunting?"

"He's hunting for souls."

"What exactly does he do with them?"

June shrugged. "Depends on what he wants to do with them. Sometimes demons eat souls, while other times they turn them into their minions by corrupting them."

"Oh."

June reached out and took my hand. I met her gaze. "You have to focus, Eliza. We need to stay on task. Death has no concept of time, but your soul is meant to die within the next few days."

"What! No one told me that."

"As the Lamb of Essence, you have never lived past your twenty-fifth year; especially not after the competition has begun. Either a demon or an angel will claim your soul soon. Kaleb and his minions will be out to kill you, and who knows what Gabriel is planning now that he has the wisdom granted to archangels. We have to have Death free you today because you might not last another."

I nodded. "So, what do we do?"

June smiled before turning serious. "I only know of one way to make an angel cry."

"And that is?"

"By playing the 'Devil's Trill' on a demon's violin."

I frowned. "By playing music?"

"It's not just any music."

"Isn't that a classical song or something?"

June nodded and began to lead me out of the alley. "Yes. It was written by a composer named Giuseppe Tartini."

"So how does that help exactly?"

"Tartini wrote the song after having a dream. In that dream, he met the devil. He offered the devil his violin, on which he played a haunting tune. Once Tartini woke from the dream, he attempted to create the same tune, and thus the 'Devil's Trill' was written. What people don't know is that it was a song the devil played after his fall from Heaven. It contains all the sorrows of the Morning Star and all of his regrets. When played on a demon's violin, it will make a demon laugh, but it will make an angel cry for the loss of one of their own. It is very rare that an angel's soul is blackened while they are in Heaven but when it happens, they mourn the loss."

I was speechless as I walked next to June. Then something she said bothered me. "You said you have to play it on a demon's violin? What is that?"

June frowned. "A demon's violin is made of gold, but only certain people can play it."

"What do you mean?"

June stopped and turned to me. "It's a demonic treasure that only high-ranking demons possess. To play it, a person's pain must be greater than the pain the violin can inflict."

"What happens if it isn't?"

She shook her head. "I don't know."

"So we're going to get Kaleb to play it?"

"No, Eliza."

"No?"

"He is forbidden to play it for an angel. It would break the rules of the truce between the angels and the demons."

I frowned. "So, who's going to play it?"

She didn't answer, but began walking again. I reached out and grabbed her hand. "June, we talked about this."

She sighed, but turned back. "I am, Eliza. I'm going to play the violin."

"THE HELL YOU ARE!"

"We don't have time for this."

"Then make time for it!"

June met my angry gaze with a patient one. "Eliza, we don't have a choice."

I frowned. "There's always a choice."

She smiled and nodded. "You're right. You made yours, now let me make mine."

I let go, but she reached out and locked our fingers together. She pulled me in the direction of an empty apartment building. No longer were we on the sidewalk just outside an alleyway. I suddenly realized that while we were speaking, June had moved us through another portal. It was reassuring that my stomach didn't flip out this time. Maybe I was getting used to it.

The abandoned building had boards covering all of the entrances, but June walked us around to the side of it and paused in front of a window. She reached out and pushed on the board covering the window and it slid out of the way.

"Come on," June whispered, and stepped through the hole. Taking a deep breath, I followed her and stepped through the opening. I expected it to be dark and cold inside but as I stepped past the threshold, a tamed heat wrapped around me and a subtle light illuminated the open space that could have been a living room once. The light was coming from candles scattered about the room.

I turned to June as she reached out for my hand again. "Are there people here?"

She nodded and whispered, "Stay next to me."

"Okay."

She pulled me into the room and led me through a hallway. Trash littered the floor, and I gasped when a rat ran across my path, disappearing into an open room. We came to a flight of stairs leading up but I hesitated when I put my weight on the first step and it gave a little too much under my foot. I tried to step back, but June wouldn't release her hold on my hand.

"Don't worry. I've got you."

I nodded and followed after her quickly. The stairs led up to another hallway with several closed doors. I could hear hushed voices coming from the other rooms as we walked past them and came to a pause by the door third on the left. June reached out and turned the knob, pushing it open.

The smell that was released from the room was a mixture of rotten food, body odor, and the result of bodily functions. I gasped, and immediately regretted it. Covering my mouth and nose, I attempted to rid myself of the vile odor but was unsuccessful. June seemed unaffected as she pulled me into the room. It was warmer than the rest of the house. I glanced around and found the source of heat and light. A small fireplace at the far end of the room was the reason for both. It was well stocked with what looked like books and newspapers. There even seemed to be clothing burning in the flames.

Letting my eyes trail around the rest of the room, I was able to see that there were old, ratty mattresses scattered about containing several people in varying states of dress. Some were completely bare, while others were partially clothed. No one seemed to mind the chill that was still in the room despite the heat of the fire.

"What—"

June held up her hand, silencing whatever questions I wanted to ask. She scanned the room before her gaze seemed to settle on a teenage boy. She pulled me in his direction. I watched as the boy whispered something into a woman's ear, all while closing her hand around an uncapped needle. The woman's eyes were empty as she plunged the needle without hesitation into the crook of her arm. Her whole body seemed to pull taught at the sudden intrusion, but as she pushed the plunger forward, she seemed to sag in some relief until she drooped, then fell back onto the mattress.

We came to a halt behind the boy and June cleared her throat, getting his attention. He looked up at us, confused for a moment, before a wicked grin spread across his face.

"Kaleb," June stated in even tones.

He chuckled and stood. His youthful face threw me off, as I was used to his mature features. The eyes that met mine were still as dark as I remembered, though. His voice was boyish and cracked a little as he spoke, as if he was just entering puberty. "June! I see you've brought me a snack."

I shuddered, and her hand tightened around mine.

"Kaleb, I've come for your treasure."

He tilted his head to the side as he studied June. "My violin?"

She nodded, and he grinned. "Has Death requested something unreasonable? I wonder what that old bastard has up his sleeve this time?"

"Your violin."

He pouted. A cruel expression on such boyish and haggard features. "You're no fun."

"Kaleb," she warned.

"Yes, my dear. I hear you. I'll lend it to you, but only until sunset."

June frowned. "Aren't you going to ask for something in return?"

He grinned. "Do you want me to?"

She didn't answer, so he continued. "June, June, June. How little you think of me. I have a good idea of what you have planned and I dare say that it will be payment enough to watch an angel shed tears. Those self-righteous winged beasts always piss me off. Let's just say that you are doing me a favor."

I glanced to June. She didn't seem convinced. I tightened my grip on her hand. "Just take it, June," I whispered to her.

She sighed but held out her hand. Kaleb smirked and snapped his fingers. A golden violin materialized in June's hand. She held it with ease, despite the heavy material it was made from. I felt a tug on my hand as she began to lead me away from the demon, but he reached out and grabbed my shoulder, stopping us.

"You do know the payment to play a song, right?"

I nodded. "Pain."

He grinned. "Be careful; it tends to be greedy."

I frowned. "I'll keep that in mind."

Kaleb released me and held his hands up in surrender. "Then have at it, kids."

June tugged on our joined hands again. "Come on, Eliza."

I let her lead me away from the demon, his haunting laughs echoing off the walls of the old house as I was led out. We weren't free from them until we stepped outside the abandoned building.

"Now, we have to go to the gallery. Gabriel is still there."

"June."

She turned to me. I glanced down at the demonic instrument. It looked harmless—normal, even—except for the fact that it was made of solid gold. Nothing would lead one to believe that it fed on the pain of the one who struck its chords. I looked back up, meeting June's gaze.

"Are you sure about this?"

"It's the only way."

I shook my head. "That's not what I asked."

She held up the violin, and I watched as her throat bobbed when she swallowed. Was she scared? Why was she so hard to read sometimes?

"You can tell me if you're afraid. I'm scared too."

She met my gaze; hers steadfast, but wary. "I'm scared. But I'm also sure."

I nodded and held up our joined hands between us. "Then we can be scared together."

June smiled. "I don't think I would mind that."

"Good, because we've made our choices. Now, let's see them through until the end."

June pulled me into her and wrapped her arm around my waist. "Are you ready?"

I leaned in and lightly kissed her lips before pulling back and smiling. She nodded, then faced forward. "Then let's finish this."

CHAPTER TWELVE

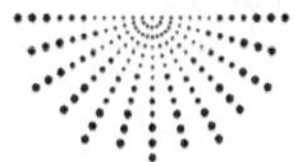

he world morphed and blurred around us until it finally stilled on the surrounding of the gallery. My stomach settled quickly, and I pulled my head off of June's shoulder. Stepping forward, June released me and looked around.

"He should be inside."

"Should we just wait until he comes out?"

"That won't be necessary. I'm here."

I turned to the entrance of Philo's only to see Gabriel exiting the gallery and making his way through the parking lot. This was it. There was no going back now. We had to get the tears, then we had to figure out how to get Kaleb's blood. Whether we would gain our freedom or not was resting on these next few hours. I just hoped my bad luck wouldn't suddenly kick in. Taking a deep breath, I yelled, "June, now!"

She placed the violin between her chin and her shoulder. I belatedly realized that a violin is usually played with a stick called a bow, but that was absent at the moment. Instead, June took a deep breath, relaxed her shoulder, and plucked one of the strings. A multitude of sounds erupted from the tiny instrument. The sound of an entire orchestra tuning at once blasted in the open air before settling on the single somber tune of a violin. Gabriel stood in place as if waiting for what was to come next. Was he expecting this?

I turned back to June and listened as she plucked several strings and a melody as haunting as it was powerful played out in the fading light of the day. The sound of the violin reverberated from the golden strings with a strength I had never known such a small instrument could wield. June's face seemed to tense in concentration as the pace at which she plucked the strings increased, and the melody played a beautiful scale.

I could feel my eyes sting as tears threatened to fall. The song carried a great deal of pain and longing. My heart clenched as I watched several emotions play out across June's face. A masculine cry caught my attention and I turned back to Gabriel, only to see the archangel kneeling on the concrete, holding his head, flickering between the young human I knew him as and the angelic being he truly was. As June reached a crescendo he cried out in agony and his body settled on the angelic form.

Wings as white as untouched snow, spanning the length of the cars next to him on each side, Gabriel seemed to be illuminated from the inside by an ethereal light that permeated outward from his very being. He groaned and fell forward, resting his hands on the ground. His wings spread their full length, stretching before folding back into his back and suddenly, only a man kneeled before me.

A sharp sound from the violin snapped me out of my daze and I quickly ran forward toward the angel, only to realize I had nothing to catch the tear in.

"Shit!" I pulled my purse forward and dug through it.

"Shit! Shit! Shit!" My hand brushed against something plastic and I grasped it, pulling it from my purse.

"Thank you!" I held a water bottle in my hand.

Emptying its contents quickly, I dropped to my knees next to Gabriel. I was shocked by the tears streaming down the man that had always seemed like a cocky asshole whenever I bumped into him. I almost felt sorry for the guy. Then I remembered that the last time I bumped into him, he tried to kill me. "Fuck it!"

I held the bottle against his face and let a few tears drop into it. I didn't know how many I needed, but after a few seconds, I stood. Would it be bad karma if I kicked an angel while he was down? Shaking my head, I ran back over to June and rested my hand on her shoulder.

"June, you can stop now."

She continued to play, and didn't even seem to register that I had spoken. "June."

I looked down at the strings of the violin and gasped. They were covered in blood. June's blood. I reached out and grabbed the violin, but she pushed me away and continued to play.

"June, stop! You're hurting yourself!"

She continued to play. Plucking the strings and covering them with her blood. I dove at her, but she sidestepped out of the way.

"Stop!"

A deep-throated laugh stopped another attempt at tackling her. I spun around, only to watch as the shadow of a red sedan morphed and grew, revealing Kaleb. His parting words rang in my ears as the demon smirked before me, *"...It tends to be greedy..."*

"You!" I stalked toward him but stopped as I remembered that he was a demon and I had no way to fight him if he decided to attack me. The only two lines of defense I had against him were currently occupied and in pain.

"Me!" he gleefully answered.

"Stop her. Stop the violin."

Kaleb grinned. "What will you give me?"

"You planned this! You planned this from the moment we took your stupid treasure."

He shrugged. "Nothing is free in this world."

"But you said—"

"My dear, why would you trust a demon? A demon without a contract is bound only by the power of his true name. You have neither, so I have broken no laws but a simple lie to a human."

"But…"

He laughed. "So, I'll ask again. What will you give me to save your lover? She'll die, you know. She'll play until the pain consumes her and madness takes over. The payment of pain the song she plays demands can only be paid in full by my lord and master. She was a fool to attempt to make such a payment, and now our dearest June will pay with her eternal sanity. But I can stop her. I can free her from the grip of the demonic treasure if you offer me something of value."

I glanced to June. *She will hate me.* I turned back to Kaleb. "I know what you want."

He smiled. His smooth voice was mocking as he ran a clawed hand through his dark locks. "And what is that?"

"You want my soul."

"Ah, indeed. You are not as simpleminded as I was led to believe. So, will you offer it? Your soul for her sanity?"

I squared my shoulders and met the dark abyss of his eyes. "I—"

"Ah!" A deep, guttural growl cut off my answer as an enraged angel flew past me and slammed into June. She cried out as a beam of light slashed at the violin in her grasp, shattering it to pieces. Gabriel stood, holding June in his grasp, with the demonic treasure at his feet. His face was blotchy and red, but his baby-blue eyes were a raging ocean as he stared down the demon in front of me.

Kaleb had the wits to take a step back. The angel walked over to me and pushed June into my grasp. I fell to the ground from her weight and watched as the archangel and demon faced off.

"Now, Gabe. I'm sure we can work this out civilly. There is a truce between our kind. You wouldn't want to be the one to break it first, now, would you?"

Gabriel sneered, "You are despicable, demon! Enough of your silver-tongued lies. This ends now!"

The angel raised his hand, revealing that the beam of light I had witnessed destroy the violin was, in fact, a blade made of light. Gabriel held it above his head and charged the demon. Kaleb attempted to morph back into the shadows but the light the angel emitted from his body blazed, dissipating all the shadows, and Gabriel slashed, slicing off the demon's right arm.

Kaleb cried out in agony and his arm sizzled as it cauterized. The light faded and the shadows quickly claimed the demon within their grasp, dragging him back into his realm. The arm landed a foot away from me, gushing blood. I laid June down on the ground and kissed her on the head. Then I ran over to the still bleeding arm and grabbed it. The limb wiggled a little, and I wanted to scream as the blood spurted everywhere. But I held it over the water bottle and let the crimson liquid gush into it, mixing with the salty tears.

As I was holding it, the limb suddenly began to sizzle. I dropped it and watched as the shadows rose to claim it as it melted into them.

"Gross," I whispered, and ran back over to June. Gabriel was standing over her, resting his hands on her shoulders.

"Leave her alone!" I yelled and attempted to push him away, but he was like a solid stone wall.

Gabriel sniggered and stood. "I was simply healing her wounds."

He stepped away, and I pulled June back into my grasp. Upon closer inspection, I confirmed the truth of his words. I looked back up. "Thank you…I guess."

The angel nodded.

I frowned up at him. "Why did you help us? You've been nothing but a jerk to me this whole time."

Gabriel smiled and shrugged. "Then let me formally apologize for my misconduct during this process. All I can say in my defense is that I was but a simple angel. I have since been promoted to the rank of an archangel, and as such, I have been granted some of the wisdom from the Cogs of Time. The way I treated the both of you was unacceptable. I hope you can one day find it in yourself to forgive my actions. I may be a celestial being, but I'm not perfect. Even angels make mistakes, especially when we are young. It's no excuse, but now that I know and understand the purpose of some things, I have come to respect the roles that you and June play in the grand scheme."

Gabriel bowed deeply before standing straight. "June is healed, and my purpose has been served. I will return both of you to Death."

"I don't know what to say."

Gabriel nodded. "Just remember that Death is neither good nor evil. He serves a purpose. Sometimes what he does seems evil, but the truth is that his greatest concern is to keep the balance. That doesn't mean he has your best interests at heart. Death is a title for a position of great importance. He will do whatever it takes to keep that title."

"I think I understand."

"Good." Then he placed his hands on both of us, and the

feeling of wrongness filled me as the world around me shifted. I closed my eyes and gripped onto June tightly. Going back to the Otherworld was way worse than traveling to different places in the physical realm. It always felt like someone was trying to rip my soul from my body only to let go at the very end.

"Ah, you have returned." The cold, apathetic voice of Death made me open my eyes.

My grip on June tightened as I met the dark gaze of Death—the man responsible for all my hardships. I held up the bottle of the combined tears and blood. "I have what you want."

He stood and moved with the grace of a cat as he stalked over to us and reached out to grab the bloody water bottle between two fingers as if it was a dirty diaper.

"Yes. You seem to have done as I requested. I suppose I should fulfill my end of the contract as well." He walked with a lazy gait that belied the power his body held that the grace hinted at. He placed the bottle on his desk and unscrewed the lid. He tipped it over, and I watched as the mixture of blood and tears poured down onto his impeccably clean desk. I gasped and watched as the wooden monstrosity morphed into a giant mouth that rose up and grabbed the bottle from Death's hand, swallowing it whole.

"The desk—"

"Now that you have signed with blood, the contract will not fade; you are under Death's dominion until Death is remade."

"Did I just make another contract?"

Bored, dark eyes met mine, and the man sighed. "Were either of those substances yours?"

I shook my head.

"Then why would you believe it was a contract made for you?"

"But you said that thing! That thing that you say!"

He nodded solemnly. "Yes. It appears I did indeed say something."

I frowned. "If it wasn't for me, then who was it for?"

Death's apathetic gaze met mine and he seemed to sink into his leather chair. "To free you from your role as the Lamb of Essence, I must put into place another contract that will prevent the demons and angels from beginning their long and boring war with each other. Did you think that everyone would be happy-go-lucky if I freed you from your duty?"

"Well, no, but—"

"But, you are now free from all contracts with me."

"I'm free?"

Death waved his hand in the air. "All contracts are nullified by Death's decree; I set you, Eliza Trust, free."

My heart stuttered, and I suddenly felt a heavy weight lift from me. A giddiness filled me as I looked down to June, who was still unconscious; but something Death said struck me, or rather something he didn't say.

"You said *I* was free. What about June?"

He shrugged. "What about her?"

I glared at the man before me. "The agreement was that both June and I would be free from the contract she first made with you."

He leveled me with the coldest look anyone has ever given me. "That was not the agreement that I made. She is still a bone walker under my service, and I have no intention of releasing her today or anytime soon. I keep up my end of all contracts I make and you, Eliza Trust, have no contract with me, and no longer have any reason to be within my realm. I will let you keep your memories, as that was stated in the contract, but I will not have a human in my presence."

He seemed to sneer the word *human* as his face twisted into an ugly frown.

"So, I ban you from the Otherworld until further notice."

"You can't—"

"Begone, human with no purpose to me or my own."

"But—"

I gasped as I felt the familiar feeling of being pulled through a portal. I gripped onto June, but she was fading as if she wasn't physical.

"June!" I screamed.

The feeling disappeared, and I was once again alone in the four walls of my apartment. I was still covered by the blood of a demon but the tears streaming down my face were my own. The last thing tying me to my soul mate was gone. I was once again torn from the woman I had come to realize meant more to me than anything else in my existence. She was gone, and I had no way of finding her again. *Banned.* I was banned from the Otherworld, the world where June resided. We were once again, worlds apart.

I SLAPPED A TWENTY DOWN ONTO THE COUNTER, ONCE AGAIN startling the teenage boy. He looked up from his phone only to take a step back in fear, probably from my expression.

"One ticket? Hold on, I'll get it for you. Just, give me a second," he croaked, and hurriedly printed off one ticket, handing it to me.

He didn't even bring up the fact that there were no tours currently running at the moment. He simply watched on in fear as I took the stairs leading down into the Underground. I took the now familiar path until I tracked down the parlor.

Quickly, I waded through the wide, crumbling opening and climbed over the bar, all but falling over myself in my haste to get to the back room, to get back to June. But as I walked behind the bar I was met with a solid stone wall instead of the wooden door I was expecting.

I stared at it numbly for a moment. A wall? Why was there a wall here? Where was the door? That bastard! That fucking bastard! My hand flew out, slapping hard against the wall. The pain didn't even register. "Damn you, Death! Damn you to Hell!" I screamed as I fell to the ground, wailing and cursing the man's impeccable suit and cold, dark eyes.

I don't know how long I sat there crying. It could have been only minutes or hours. It didn't matter much. The only thing that mattered to me had been ripped from my grasp and held out of reach forever. It wasn't until I felt warm hands on my shoulders that I realized I was being led back up the stairs and back into the lobby.

The boy at the counter must have told someone that I went downstairs. I looked at the woman that was leading me and saw that it was the same woman that had led the tour the last time I visited the Underground. She was telling me something as she led me into a bathroom, but I just continued to cry. She must have thought I was insane, but she patiently stayed with me until my tears dried up, then handed me a box of tissues. Once I had cleaned up a little bit, she gave me my money back and walked me the few blocks to the bus stop.

"You'll be all right, miss," she whispered before gently squeezing my hand and walking away.

I took the bus back to my apartment in a state of numbness. It wasn't until I was lying in bed that night that the reality finally sank in. I was never going to see June again. I was once again alone in the world. Death had taken from me my most important person, and he was never going to let her go. Was my freedom really worth the cost of never seeing her again? If I could do it over again, would I? Would I give up a chance at a normal life to be with her again? In a heartbeat! I drifted off to sleep cursing him, even as I silently begged him to set her free.

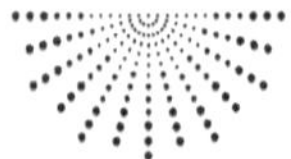

CHAPTER THIRTEEN

I knocked, and Angela answered the door with a smile.

"Eliza, you made it! Happy Thanksgiving! Come on in. May just pulled the turkey out."

The Asian woman all but dragged me into the warm house. The smells of Thanksgiving dinner surrounded me, making my mouth instantly water as I was dragged into the living room that was filled with screaming children chasing each other and May and Peter's rambunctious family.

"Angela, slow down!" I laughed as my friend dragged me through the living room, past the dining room, and into the kitchen where May was chopping potatoes.

"Look who's finally here!"

May looked up, and I winced as an image of her chopping off a finger flitted through my mind. "Stop chopping!" I said.

May laughed and placed the knife down before reaching out and pulling me into a bone-crushing hug. "Eliza! I wasn't sure if you would make it!"

She released me, and I shrugged. "Wouldn't miss it for the world."

She smiled and picked up the knife again. "Peter is in the game room. Grab a beer and join in. Angela will introduce you to all the non-crazy relatives. I'll warn you now to stay away from my aunt Bertha. She'll talk to you about her millions of cats for hours."

I chuckled. "Duly noted."

Angela tugged on my hand. "I'll take her to Peter. Is dinner almost ready?"

May held the knife up to point it at us. "Ask me again, and things will get very dangerous very quickly."

I gulped. "I think I'll get that beer you mentioned."

Her face lit up with a smile. "Of course! They're in the cooler downstairs in the game room."

"May, have you started the potatoes yet?" an older woman asked as she carried a tray of steaming yams past us.

"I'm on it, Mom. Can you help me chop?"

"Sure."

"Now, shoo! You two. You're distracting me." May waved the knife around and Angela and I hurriedly left the kitchen.

We were dodging tumbling children as we made our way to the stairs. "Remind me to never ask May a question while she has a sharp knife in her hand."

Angela chuckled. "You should know that the short ones are the ones to watch out for."

I laughed, and we made our way down to the game room. Peter was shooting pool with three other men. They were his older brothers, if I remembered right. The television was on with the football game, and boos along with the appropriate cheers could be heard in the background. Peter looked up as Angela and I entered the room.

"Hey, Eliza! You made it." He came over and pulled me into a bear hug.

I laughed as he let me go. "Hey, Peter. I wouldn't miss this for the world."

He smiled. "You know what? I think you need a beer. Can't have a party without one, you know?"

I nodded and followed him into the small kitchenette where they kept the cooler. I looked around at the basement, which I personally would call a man cave. "Is this where you go when May puts you in the doghouse?" I asked.

He chuckled. "Something like that. I also come down of my own volition. Every guy needs his own space just to cool off. May has a crafts room upstairs. She only comes down here for movie night. Says the lighting down here depresses her otherwise."

Angela grabbed a Samuel Adams and laughed. "I don't blame her. It seriously is a cave down here."

"Hey, there are lights! It isn't that bad." Peter pulled out a bottle and popped the cap off with the bottle opener on the counter before handing me the beer.

"It is a bit dark down here," I played along.

"It's a basement!"

Angela and I laughed as he pouted, then the Asian woman moved in closer to him and whispered, "So, Pete. Which one of your brothers is single?"

He frowned. "Seriously? I thought we went over this. They are all jerks."

Angela nodded patiently, and I smirked. He really should learn that no man is off her radar. "I know we talked, and I assure you that I attempted to listen, but all I could hear was how protective you are of your older, more sexy, brothers. Now, which one is single? I need to start working one over now so that by the end of the dinner I can drag one home with me, or at least get a number."

"Angela—"

She gave him a deadpan look. "Peter."

He sighed. "Fine. I don't know why I even try. Paul is single right now. He just got out of a long relationship. But

I'll warn you, Angela; he's not looking for anything serious right now."

She shrugged. "Who said I was? So, which one is Paul?"

Peter nodded his head in the direction of the pool table. "He's the second-youngest, and the one taking a shot right now."

"Hmm, nice ass."

"Angela!"

She looked at him. "What? He has one."

"He's my brother!" Peter all but whined.

Angela gave him a once-over before smirking. "I wouldn't have guessed." Then she sashayed over to the pool table, and Peter grumbled under his breath.

I took a swig and smiled. I missed these guys! Peter pulled out another beer, then mentioned something about going to see May before walking off with a deep frown. I leaned back against the counter and took another drink.

It's strange how I could be in a room filled with people that I care about yet still feel so alone. Almost like being invisible, even when I'm in plain sight. When I was with June, it always felt like I was the center of her universe, and she was the sun that I orbited around. Now, my sun was gone, and I felt an emptiness in my chest that I didn't think I could ever fill. In this lifetime I had only known her for a little over a month, and yet she quickly became the closest thing I had to a real family. She was a person that knew all of my faults and still loved me despite them. How was I supposed to keep moving forward without her?

I watched Angela giggle at something Paul said and twirl a lock of her hair around a finger. She had always been able to have fun with another person no matter how briefly she knew them. Peter and May were able to as well. They were all able to build bonds effortlessly, when I felt like all I ever did was break them. My bonds were like weeping wounds, as they all ended suddenly and without warning. How was I supposed to make a place for myself in this world when everyone I loved kept dying or disappearing from my life?

I was brought back to the present by someone poking me in my shoulder. I looked up from my beer and into May's eyes. She smiled. "Dinner is ready. Are you coming back upstairs?"

I looked around the room and noticed that it was empty. Nodding, I slowly followed May back into the dining room and couldn't help the smile that spread across my face to see that Angela had saved me a seat between her and May.

Taking my seat between two good friends, a thought occurred to me. Not all of my bonds were broken. In fact, the ones that had survived were stronger than ever. I had friends that had become my family. If I was going to survive this constant ache in my chest, it was going to be because they supported me. I needed to tell them what I could; what they would understand. I needed to tell them because they were my family, even if it wasn't by blood, and they had stuck with me through thick and thin.

"Hey, Eliza, pass the cranberry sauce!" Peter said as he handed me the basket of rolls while attempting to shove one in his mouth at the same time. I giggled and picked up the requested dish. It is said that you don't get to choose your family, but I wouldn't trade them in for the world.

"I'm so stuffed," I whined as I patted my swollen belly.

Peter laughed and passed an open Samuel Adams Octoberfest over to me. "Enough room for a beer, I hope?"

I took the offered drink. "There's always room for one more beer. Except for when I'm puking my guts out. That's when I've reached my limit."

Angela snorted. "That's some limit."

I smirked. "You would know."

May snickered. "I'm glad you all liked it. It was my first time leading the cooking. It's nice to know I pulled it off and it is appreciated."

I burped. "Much appreciated."

They all laughed.

Peter cleared his throat. "So, have you been all right lately, Eliza?"

May smacked him on the arm. I frowned. "What do you mean?"

May interrupted before he could answer. "What Peter is trying to say is that you've seemed distant lately. We were all wondering if something was going on."

"Like a secret lover!" Angela wiggled her eyebrows.

I studied my beer for a moment. Should I tell them? What could it hurt? Everything was over now. It might as well have all been a really vivid dream. I shrugged and took a drink before answering. "There was a secret lover."

Angela sprayed her drink and May cringed. "Eww."

"What!" Peter yelled.

Angela turned to me. "You are dating someone?"

I nodded. "Well, I was. Yeah."

Peter frowned. "Wait, was?"

I looked up and met the stunned faces of my closest friends. "Yeah. You could even say she was my soul mate."

I could feel the tears falling, even though I had no energy to stop them.

"Oh, Eliza." Angela moved over next to me and pulled me into a hug. "What happened?"

"We just weren't meant to be, I guess." I hiccupped.

Peter interrupted. "Wait. Did you say *she*?"

I nodded. "Yeah. Her name was June, and I think I was in love with her."

"Shhh, it's okay, Eliza." Angela pulled me closer.

"You're gay?" Peter said.

May slapped him on the arm again. "Would you shut up, captain obvious? Can't you see she's torn up about this woman?"

"Hold up. How come none of you are surprised that Eliza is a lesbian?"

I looked up at Angela and then to May. "Neither of you seem very surprised."

Angela chuckled. "We both just figured you were in denial. That's why you never dated in college. I mean, come on, Eliza. You never even talked about guys when May or I would gush about them."

I frowned. "But I never talked about girls, either."

May shrugged. "We figured either you were a late bloomer and were going to find a great guy one day or you were gay. Either way, we all love you, Eliza. I just want you to know that we would never stop talking to you just because you like the fairer sex."

"She's a lesbian."

Angela growled, "Peter, would you shut up!"

He turned to me. "Are you telling me that I could have dated a lesbian and had hot threesomes in college and no one told me!"

"Peter!" May smacked him in the face this time, snapping him out of whatever daydreams he was having. He blushed. "Sorry. I just had a moment. It's passed."

I laughed even as I gasped. "You guys are great. I don't know what I would do without you."

"Have hot lesbian sex."

"Peter!" both Angela and May yelled.

"Sorry."

Angela turned back to me. "Do you want to talk about her?"

I shook my head. "Not right now. It's still too fresh. I just…I just miss her so much. I couldn't tell her how I really felt before she left. If I could just get one more chance to see her, I would give anything to tell her how I truly feel."

Angela kissed the top of my head. "I'm sorry, Eliza."

"Where did she go? Is there any way we can reach her?" May asked.

I shook my head. "She's practically in another world."

May nodded. "I'm sorry too, Eliza. The first is always the hardest, especially when it was so deep."

"Well." Peter stood up. "How about we get smashed? I have Crown in a cupboard around here somewhere. I also hid a bottle of birthday cake vodka under the couch."

I laughed. "I like the sound of that."

We all laughed before Angela turned to me. "Just remember, Eliza, you're never alone. We've always got your back."

"Thank you. I won't forget again."

Angela smiled. "Good, because you don't want me to go crazy best friend on you if you do. Because you know I'm still pissed I didn't hear about this June girl before. I could have brought over pints of chocolate ice cream and we could have hit the chick flicks."

I laughed. "I know, Angela. I'll make sure you're in the loop next time."

"You'd better."

"Okay, enough heart to heart. I say we blast some emo rock loud enough to wake the grandparents. Let's get smashed!"

May turned him around to meet her gaze. "Peter! We are not going to do that."

He frowned. "We're not?"

"No. We are going to play some emo rock softly in the background so that we don't wake anyone up because my mom is sleeping upstairs in the guest room. Do you remember what happened last time you woke her up in the middle of the night?"

"Um, it's a bit blurry."

She nodded solemnly. "Yes, I feared it would be. You don't remember, but she pushed you down the stairs. It was bloody. I thought I lost you for a moment. It was touch and go at the hospital for a while."

"Really?"

"Yes. So how about you go and find that vodka and Crown and us girls will set up the music?"

He nodded with a confused look on his face. "Yeah, sure. Are you sure that's what happened? I think I would remember something like that."

"No, honey. You hit your head pretty hard. The doctor said you might not remember it."

"Yeah, okay. I'll get the drinks and be back in a minute."

"Thanks, sweetie."

Peter walked away, and May stood motioning for us to follow her. She led us over to the kitchenette where her cell phone and small Bluetooth speakers were.

"Did that really happen?" I asked.

May smirked but shook her head. "No. It was worse. He came home pissed drunk after a night out on the town with his brothers and woke up my mom, who was visiting at the time. She doesn't think too clearly when she's woken up in the middle of the night. It has to do with the sleeping pills she takes. You know how older people get insomnia."

I nodded and watched as she flicked through her playlist. "And?"

"Well, she came down the stairs screaming bloody murder, practically butt naked. She thought he was a burglar. She chased him out of the house with a lamp. We found him the next morning in the park, practically frozen. It was sometime in December."

"Damn, May. Are all the women crazy in your family?" Angela asked.

May looked up at her and frowned. "What are you saying?"

"Nothing. I was saying nothing!" Angela held up her hands in surrender.

May smiled and laughed. "Just kidding!"

She turned back to the speaker and indie rock music played softly in the background. I gave Angela a look and giggled at the pure terror on her face. She always did say the short ones were the ones you had to watch out for.

THE BLARING SOUND OF ROCK MUSIC WAS LIKE A DRILL IN MY head as it broke the silence of the morning.

"Oh my God! Someone turn it off!" Angela's voice called out into the darkness of the basement.

I crawled over to where I had dropped my purse the night before and dug through it, pulling out my cell phone. I didn't even have the mind to check my caller ID before I answered it.

"Hello?" My voice cracked and was scratching, causing me to cough.

"Eliza! I have wonderful news!"

"Henry?" Oh God! Did I miss a meeting?

"Yes, of course, dear. Are you not quite awake yet? That's all right; I'll just talk and you listen."

"Okay," I whispered, and moved to sit up off the floor. I shivered as the sleeping bag fell down and quickly pulled it back up. The basement didn't get good heating.

"I've spoken with several of our patrons, and it has been decided upon that we have a teaser of your artwork this week after the holiday has ended. They want to see what you have to offer, and it will give us a great chance to stir some excitement for your future show next year. I'm thinking the day after Black Friday. What do you think?"

"Saturday?"

"Yes, dear. You must have had a rough night. In case you didn't know, today is Friday. So, I was speaking about tomorrow."

"Yeah, okay. We can do whatever you want, Henry."

"Great! This is great news. I will be expecting to see you early tomorrow to work out the details; say, about seven in the morning?"

I swallowed thickly. Shit, what was I supposed to say? My head throbbed. Thinking was not a good idea right now. "Sure."

"This is going to be wondrous! I'll see you tomorrow. Please, don't be late. We have much to accomplish before the show later that evening."

"Okay." I was already beginning to fall asleep again as my hangover overloaded my brain. I don't know if I hung up or if he did, but it was only seconds later that I was back into the warm abyss of the dream world.

CHAPTER FOURTEEN

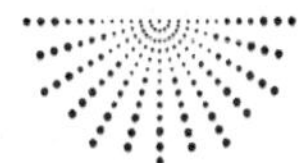

"Remind me again why I let you two talk me into shopping on Black Friday, the craziest day of the year," I croaked as I dropped two aspirin into my hand and took them with a swig of water from my bottle.

"Because we are awesome and wonderful and you love us, so you will do anything to make us happy," Angela said.

I shook my head. "More like because you threatened to withhold my Christmas presents if I didn't come with you." I groaned. I was still nursing a hangover.

May looped her arm through mine and smiled. "That too."

"Where to first, ladies? Momma wants a new pair of high heels!"

"Oh God! She's calling herself names again. That is never a good sign." I moaned, and May giggled beside me.

"I still need to buy Peter his gift," May said, and began dragging me toward Best Buy.

"You haven't bought one yet?" I asked.

She shook her head. "Are you finished with your Christmas shopping?"

"No, not yet. I've been busy lately, and haven't really gotten the chance to do much." Even as I spoke, memories from the past few days flitted through my mind. I really did have an eventful last few days. From fighting angels to making deals with demons…how was one supposed to find time to Christmas shop? I sighed. Well, I guess I had all the time in the world now that I was free from it all. Or at least the few weeks until the holiday. May interrupted my thoughts.

"What are your plans for Christmas and New Year's?"

I shrugged. "Nothing yet. Why?"

She smiled at me. "I just wanted to make sure you knew that you were welcome to spend it with Peter and me. I don't know what Angela has planned yet but she is also invited. We were thinking about going to some New Year's parties this time. Peter has a few colleagues that are throwing some that are supposed to be a bit crazy."

I smiled. "Thanks, May. I think I might take you up on that offer. It would suck to bring in the New Year alone."

She nodded. "It's bad luck, too."

I chuckled just as Angela ran to catch up with us once she figured out we weren't following her anymore. "Jeez, guys! Just walk away without me why don't you?"

May smirked. "We didn't want to interrupt your shoe fantasies."

I opened my mouth to give her another dig when a masculine voice interrupted whatever I was about to say. "Eliza? Eliza Trust, is that you?"

I spun around, only to come face-to-face with George Crane, my old boss. "Mr. Crane?"

His face lit up with a grin. "It is you! What a coincidence."

"Yeah…" I trailed off. *What should I even say in a situation like this, and why the hell does he look so happy to see me?*

"This is great!"

I frowned. "Yeah, it's nice to see you again, Mr. Crane."

He walked closer so we could speak without yelling. "I was just thinking about you."

"You were?"

He held out his hand. "Ms. Trust, you have no idea how we've missed you at the company."

"You have?" Now I was confused.

"I admit that I may have overreacted when I fired you so quickly. So, I would like to personally offer you your old position in the company back. Jacob has been a nightmare, and hasn't lived up to even one-third of my expectations. He just can't keep up with the work you could produce when you were there. Jacob has since left the company. I would be overjoyed if you would come work for us again."

I looked down at the offered hand, then looked up to meet the smiling face of my old boss. Taking a deep breath, I answered in my most polite of tones. "You know, Mr. Crane, had you asked me a month ago I would have jumped at the opportunity, but the truth is that I've since moved on. I have a show coming up at Philo's."

"The gallery?" he asked. A little bit of awe had entered his voice.

"Yes, sir. It's a great opportunity, and I've decided to pursue a career in the arts. I've had some success, and I plan to continue moving forward with that career choice. So, I'm sorry to say that I will have to decline your offer for my old position, but I would like to invite you to come to my show next year. I would even call it an eye-opening experience."

His face fell slightly. "Oh, I'm sorry to hear that. I might just take you up on your offer, though. My wife is a regular at Philo's. She dabbles with sculpting and such. Well, then, I wish you the best with your endeavors and with your holiday shopping. Good day, ladies." He nodded to both May and Angela before walking away.

"Oh my gosh!" Angela yelled and pulled me into a bone-crushing hug. "You were amazing!"

"Angela! You're choking me."

She let go. "Oh, sorry. I'm just so proud of you! Did you see his face? He was speechless! How many people tell him no after he offers them a job? You were badass!"

I laughed. "You could say that I've learned my value."

Angela pulled me into another hug. "It's about damn time you did."

I smiled. "Yeah, it really is."

"So, shopping?" May interrupted.

I smirked at her and nodded. "Sure. But I'm getting ice cream before I go home."

May frowned. "But it's November."

"That doesn't mean anything. Ice cream is a year-round snack. It's like chocolate or alcohol or weed—"

I slapped my hand over Angela's mouth. "We get it, Angela. Ice cream is great, and I want some tonight, so I'm going to buy some on my way home, and that's final."

I pulled my hand away to reveal a wide smile. I got a sinking feeling just as she opened her mouth and yelled, "Girl party!"

I groaned as May tried to quiet her down. We were getting strange looks from the people around us, and Angela began to do her victory dance. I shouldn't have said anything! *There goes my quiet night to mope by myself.* Angela was going to want to shop all day, then party all night. She might even make us do a marathon of *Friends*. I shuddered at the thought.

AFTER THE BRIEF MEETING WITH HENRY IN THE MORNING AND a mad dash with Angela trying to get all my artwork safely transported to Philo's for the show in the evening, I was reaching my limit of ass-kissing for the day. Philo's was packed with VIPs and the odd reporter or two that was going to help with the promotion for the show next year by beginning the hype now. I was both excited and terrified for the future, but mostly, I was just exhausted.

Henry had allowed me to invite a few of my friends, and of course they all said they would show up sometime throughout the day. Angela had helped me set up earlier and said she would come back during the show so she could try and "snag herself some rich man candy." Her words, not mine. I was desperately searching for a server to grab a glass of wine from when the sound of someone clearing their throat drew my attention.

I turned around to see Gabriel holding out a glass filled with white wine. I hesitated a moment, and he smiled before pushing it into my hand. "Don't worry. I don't bite."

"Gabe, why are you here?" I sipped at my drink, trying to still my racing heartbeat.

He shrugged. "I'm a patron here."

I frowned. "I thought that was your cover."

He nodded. "It was."

When he didn't continue, I felt my panic start to build. "So, why are you here?"

Gabriel looked around before meeting my gaze. His baby blues were clear as a summer's day, but his face held a graveness that unsettled me. "Eliza, I'm here for you."

I took a step back. "I thought—"

He shook his head. "Not for that reason."

"Then why? I don't want any more of your games, Gabe. Why are you here?"

He nodded and took a step forward. "I know things. And

some of the things I have come to learn have unsettled me a great deal."

I whispered, "What things?"

He frowned. "That you are important."

"I'm finished with all of that. Death said—"

Gabriel shook his head. "Death can't be trusted."

My heart began to race. "What are you saying?"

Finally, he smiled and took a step back. "I just want you to know that even if you can't trust Death, you can trust me. When the time comes, I hope you seek me out for help. I'm not your enemy."

"I don't understand what you're saying, Gabe. Why would I need your help?"

"Because, Eliza. One day, you're going to find yourself in a situation where you have no one left to turn to. At that moment, I want you to remember me and know that I am willing to help you."

"At what cost? What will I have to give for that help?" I demanded.

He frowned. "Nothing. You won't have to give me anything."

"Why—"

He shook his head, and I felt someone tap my shoulder. I turned around to see Angela, May, and Peter, all dressed in their best evening gowns and suit. "Eliza! This is wonderful!" May pulled me into a hug.

"Hey, guys. I'm glad you could make it. Can you just hold on one second, though? I'm talking to someone." I pulled back and turned to Gabe. He was gone.

"Who were you speaking with?" Angela asked when I turned back to them.

I shook my head and frowned. "No one, I guess. Sorry."

Angela perked up and pulled me into a hug as well. "So, how does it feel to be famous?"

I gave a nervous laugh, still trying to shake off the horrible feeling Gabriel left me with. What did he mean when he said I would need his help? I thought it was all over…

"Eliza?"

I shook my head to clear it and smiled. "I'm not famous yet."

"You practically are! So, point me in the direction of the richest bachelor so I can work my magic," Angela gushed.

"Have you no shame, woman?" Peter whispered.

Angela smirked, "I'm hot. What do I have to be ashamed about?"

He shook his head, and I laughed before leading them around and introducing them to a few people. We split up after a while. Angela was chatting up a handsome, six-foot bachelor while Peter and May were checking out some of the other rooms. I strolled around idly until I came to a stop in front of a painting. Looking up, I was once again caught in the gunmetal grays of my Grim Reaper. But this time, instead of the mysterious feeling they usually evoked, all I felt was a constant ache in my chest as my heart clenched in longing. Would I ever look upon the real person again? Or would I have to wait until the end of eternity?

I felt a presence come up beside me and I looked to my left to see Jessica, Henry's assistant. She didn't meet my gaze, but smirked at the painting of June.

"Jess, right?" I sniffed. I didn't realize I was so close to crying again.

She turned to me. "Eliza."

"Are you looking for Henry? I think I saw him walk that way." I pointed to my right.

She shook her head. "Actually, I was looking for you."

"For me?"

She nodded and turned back to the painting. "My name…"

"What?"

Jessica smirked. "June never told you the name of the person that told her about your opportunity all those centuries ago. Your one chance."

"What are you talking about?" Now, I was confused. This woman always had a way of catching me off guard.

She shrugged. "It's no matter. I just wanted to pay my respects and give you some advice before I'm gone. We won't be meeting again for a long while."

I frowned. "I don't—"

She cut me off. "It's funny, isn't it?"

"What is?"

Jessica met my gaze, and I gasped. Her eyes sparkled like a summer night's sky. It was like looking into a constellation.

I gasped. "What are you?"

She smirked and held out her hand. "Jessica, third sister to The Fate. A pleasure."

I hesitated, remembering what happened the last time we shook hands. She chuckled. "I see you've learned your lesson."

"What do you want? I'm free from my fate as the Lamb of Essence. What business do you have with me?"

Jessica shook her head, smiling. "Like I said, I just wanted to say goodbye. I'm leaving, and you will only remember me as Henry's assistant. I have served my purpose to my sister."

I frowned. "What does she want with me?"

She shrugged. "I'm but a part of the whole. Only The Fate is all-knowing. As her sister, I merely do her bidding."

Sighing, I looked back at the painting and shivered. There was a chill flowing through the gallery. I rubbed my arms to get some warmth back into them. "You said it is funny. What is funny?"

I saw her nod in approval out of the corner of my eye.

"That one can spend lifetimes trying to defy Fate. But the truth is that one does not defy Fate, they simply do her bidding, thinking they have."

I nodded. "Is life just some game for the powers that be to move us, their pawns, into place with their steady, all-powerful hands without a care for our feelings and emotions? Can we not escape our destiny? Are we cursed to be forever moved by unstoppable forces?"

Jessica shrugged. "What a silly question to ask another pawn."

"Yeah, sorry."

We stood in silence for a moment. Then she spoke again. "Do you have what it takes?"

I turned to her. "What do you mean?"

She smirked. "Can you become the immovable object that the unstoppable forces encounter? Or will you continue to be moved by those steady hands that care little of how you feel?"

I studied the woman next to me. Her eyes were filled with stars, her skin dark, and her hair styled in long ringlets. She was beautiful in her own right, but she was also trapped. Like me, she was another piece on the board. Her eyes told me she couldn't completely be trusted because despite being a piece she was also a player, and if I wasn't careful, she would be moving me one day.

I nodded. "One day, maybe."

Jessica laughed. "One day, then. Now, I must be off. I've stayed a bit longer than I planned. Take care of yourself, Eliza. There is still much for you to do."

"I'll keep that in mind."

"Please do." She smiled and walked out of my life. Another supernatural being leaving my life like a ghost only I could remember.

I sighed and went to find Henry. He was chatting up a future patron. I interrupted as politely as I could. "Henry?"

He turned to me, and his face immediately lit up with excitement. "Eliza! I was just speaking with Julia and Frank about how wonderful it is to show your artwork here."

I smiled at the two people and turned back to Henry. "That's great, but I just wanted to tell you that I have an emergency and have to leave a bit earlier than expected."

His face fell slightly. "Oh, that's a shame. There were still so many people I was going to introduce you to."

"Maybe some other time."

"Are you sure you can't stay longer? I can just do some quick introductions."

I shook my head. "I'm afraid I must decline."

"But, my dear, it will only take a moment."

Jeez, this guy was stubborn! I placed my hand on my stomach and made the best sick face I could muster without showing my annoyance. "The truth is that I seem to have eaten something that doesn't wholly agree with me."

His face lit with understanding. "Oh! I see. Well then, please do what you must. I'll hold the fort down here, so to speak." He rubbed his chin awkwardly.

I nodded and whispered to the two people he was speaking with, "I'd stay away from the tuna salad, if you know what I mean."

A look of disgust settled on their faces and they nodded as I left with a pleased look on my face. I was shuffling a few things around in my purse as I walked through the parking lot. I had been taking the bus regularly again—it was something I was proud of—when I heard a throat clear. I stopped and stared.

Her hair swayed in the breeze and her tan leather jacket was pulled tightly around her small frame. The black leather jacket she had given to me was wrapped around my own shoulders. I had worn it despite the fact that it clashed with my outfit. I just wanted to keep a part of her close to me at all times. Her soft voice cut through my shock. "I thought you might need a ride." She stood from where she was leaning against her black Camaro and held out her hand.

Without hesitation, I jogged the few steps to close the distance between us and grasped it, letting her pull me into her. Then her hot mouth was on mine, our tongues locked in an age-old dance. I wrapped my arms around her neck, burying my fingers into her white-gold locks. She pulled my hips to meet hers. It was unlike any kiss we had ever shared. It was soft and simple, and it was slow and unhurried. We took our time saying hello after that terrible goodbye that was forced upon us. When we pulled away from each other, it was slowly and breathlessly.

"June, how...?" I whispered, meeting her stormy gaze.

She shook her head and gave me a small smile. "Let me take you home. I can't stay long."

My grasp around her neck tightened. "You're going to leave again?"

She nodded. "I'm in the middle of a job, but I..."

"What?"

"I just had to see you."

I smiled. I needed to say it. Who knew when I would see her again? This might truly be my last chance, and it would be my greatest regret never to tell her how I truly feel. To never let her hear the depth of my feeling for her not as a beautiful lie, but as the honest to God truth. "I love you, June West. More than life itself. I just wanted you to know."

She drew me closer and whispered against my lips, "I do, I have, and I always will."

TEASER: COGS OF TIME

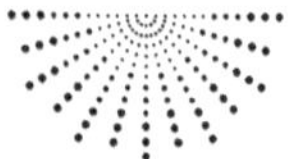

I was having a great dream when the feeling of warmth and the smell of burnt cinnamon brought me back to reality. I smiled lazily as soft lips trailed down the side of my neck before finding a sensitive spot and lightly nibbling. A silky tongue snaked out to run along the scar on my neck. She sucked a moment above it before sliding back down to pay it more attention. She never shied away from the scar. If anything, she liked to give it more attention, to let me know that it didn't affect my beauty in her eyes.

"Mmm, June," I sighed.

I felt her smile against my skin as her hands trailed up under my pajama shirt. Her blunt nails scraped lightly, causing me to shiver in anticipation.

"June," I moaned as her tongue found the sensitive spot behind my ear and her hand teased around my nipple. I arched into her touch, wanting full contact, and she swallowed my wanton moan as her mouth claimed my own. Her tongue slid in without asking and met mine, sliding and moving in an age-old dance.

She moaned and finally pinched my nipple as our hips

met and a hard thigh slid between my legs. I only slept in my underwear and a pajama shirt so when her thigh found my center, she let out a guttural moan.

"You're so hot for me, Eliza."

I whined as her mouth left mine to trail hot, wet kisses down my neck until she reached my collarbone, where she bit down lightly and sucked a moment before continuing her exploration. Her hands deftly undid the buttons of my top. She paused to meet my gaze, and I gasped as her gray eyes smoldered like burnt embers as she smirked up at me. I threaded my fingers through her hair and sighed. "June."

She bent down and kissed my collarbone again before opening my shirt. The cold air made me shiver, and she wasted no time in claiming my neglected nipple into the warm cavern of her mouth. I moaned and arched into her rubbing my sex against her leg, slickening it with my want.

"More, June!" I whined as her tongue circled my nipple. I felt her smile against me before teasing the hard nub with her teeth while her other hand pinched its twin. I was so hot as I rubbed faster against the thigh between my legs. The rough material of her jeans was teasing the bundle of nerves every time it rubbed just right and sent a shock of pleasure through my system.

"More, June. I want more!" I gasped when her hand ghosted across my stomach and down to my hips, where she slowed my desperate grinding.

"Someone's impatient today," she chuckled.

"June!" I whined, and she had the nerve to smirk up at me while she trailed open kisses down my stomach, slightly circling my belly button before making her way to my hips, where she paused to suck for a moment.

I jerked up when her tongue slid just above the waistband of my boy boxers, a gag gift from Angela after I came out to her. She said I'd probably wear the pants in the relationship. She obviously hadn't met June.

"Yes," I sighed as she used her teeth to pull down my underwear.

My door flew open. "Morning, Eliza! I brought coffee!"

"Fuck!" I yelled as my friend barged into my bedroom.

"Why are you naked?" she asked as she took a sip from her coffee.

Once again, June had portal-shifted in the middle of our lovemaking to avoid being seen, leaving me frustrated and pissed off. I pulled my pajama top securely around me and pulled my covers up. "What are you doing here, Angela?" I asked between gritted teeth.

She shook the hand that had the to-go cup in it. "Coffee?"

I gave her an annoyed look. "And?"

She frowned. "You forgot."

"Forgot what?"

"We are all supposed to go out today. Today's your birthday, Eliza!"

I ran a hand through my tousled hair. "Shit."

"Come on, birthday girl. Get ready. I'll tell May and Peter that you're coming down."

"Okay. Sorry, Ang."

"It's no problem."

I smiled and climbed out of bed, but was stopped by Angela's voice. "Oh, and Eliza?"

"Yeah?"

She pointed at my neck. "You might want to cover that up if you don't want May asking a bunch of questions."

My hand flew up to my neck. Dammit! I told her not to leave marks. I sighed. "I will. Thanks, Angela."

She smirked. "We're going to have a talk later. But right now, you have to get ready. May and I have a busy day planned for you."

I groaned. They always went overboard on things like this. "Fine, I'm getting up."

"Good! I'll be downstairs!" Angela called out over her shoulder as she left my bedroom, setting the coffee down on my dresser on her way out. I was beginning to regret giving her a spare key. She had horrible timing, and I didn't think my body could handle much more torture.

"This is all your fault, June," I whispered, and heard a faint laugh. Sighing, I climbed out of bed and grabbing some clothes, made my way to the shower. I would just have to take care of it myself this time. Damn, Angela!

AUTHOR'S NOTE

Hi! I hope you enjoyed this book, I had a lot of fun writing it. If you're interested in keeping up with the latest published books in this series and others, consider joining my email list.

Click Here!

Thank you,
   Idella Breen

ALSO BY IDELLA BREEN

<u>The Dance of The Firefly</u>
When The Clock Strikes Nothing

<u>Fire& Ice:</u>
Blood Bound

Soul Awakened

Lover Eternal/Adventures of Elena the Werewolf

Pack Mentality

The King of Brimstone and Bones

<u>Blood & Ember:</u>
Blood Eternal: Book One of Salt

<u>Witch Twin Chronicles:</u>
Unrestricted Magic

<u>Eternal Soul Trilogy:</u>
Bone Walker

<u>Water & Bone:</u>
The Girl Who Leapt Worlds

<u>Novellas:</u>
Feeders and Bleeders

Descent